Campfire
Tales MIDWEST

Campfire Tales

Mike Ricksecker

MIDWEST

Schiffer Publishing Ltd

4880 Lower Valley Road • Atglen, PA 19310

Designed by Danielle D. Farmer
Type set in Decaying/Helvetica Neue LT Pro/Titan/After Shok

ISBN: 978-0-7643-4771-9
Printed in The United States

Schiffer Books are available at special discounts for bulk purchases for sales promotions or premiums. Special editions, including personalized covers, corporate imprints, and excerpts can be created in large quantities for special needs. For more information contact the publisher:

Published by Schiffer Publishing, Ltd.
4880 Lower Valley Road
Atglen, PA 19310
Phone: (610) 593-1777; Fax: (610) 593-2002
E-mail: Info@schifferbooks.com

For the largest selection of fine reference books on this and related subjects, please visit our website at **www.schifferbooks.com.**
We are always looking for people to write books on new and related subjects. If you have an idea for a book, please contact us at
proposals@schifferbooks.com.

This book may be purchased from the publisher.
Please try your bookstore first.
You may write for a free catalog.

PHOTO CREDITS:
"Campfire with tent in background for camping scene" © Lane Erickson. Image from BigStockPhoto.com.
"Burnt Paper" © Dana Rothstein. Image from BigStockPhoto.com.
"Fire" © Vitaliy Pakhnyushchyy. Image from BigStockPhoto.com.
"Burned Marshmallow Isolated On White" © Joe Belanger. Image from BigStockPhoto.com.
"Old Fuel" © JP Nel. Image from BigStockPhoto.com

OTHER BOOKS BY THIS AUTHOR:

Ghosts and Legends of Oklahoma
978-0-7643-3943-1 $16.99

Ghosts of Maryland
978-0-7643-3423-8 $14.99

To Grandma and Grandpa Ricksecker

The author appreciates the invaluable help and/or inspiration of the following people and organizations:

Linda McCauley, Rick Hayes, Marley Gibson, Patrick Burns, Chaffee Crossing Historic District, Belvoir Winery, Beth Meyers, Mary Briggs, Nick Spantgos, Lee Ehrlich, Solvej Jordahl, Chessly Nesci, AnnMarie Barrett, Dinah Roseberry, the Indian Chief gang (Toni, Mindy, and Matt circa 1985), Society of the Haunted, Vanessa Hogle, Johnny Longan, Robbie Thomas, Robert Rothschild, Max King, Gail Ricksecker (for my first ghost book: *Yankee Ghosts* by Hans Holzer), Collin Ricksecker, Arielle Ricksecker, Chase Ricksecker, Cameron Ricksecker, Margaret Ehrlich, Patrick Rosnack—and to Heather Sinclair for the continued motivation and support to complete this work during an extremely difficult time of my life.

The idea to write a collection of fictional tales based on real history and legends of the Midwest enthralled me. By nature, I've always been a fiction writer, even back to my youngest days, when I used to write little detective stories in the second grade. The idea of creating my own legends from the real history of the land fascinated me. After all, I'd done it before. ("The Legend Beneath the Coal Bin" in Chapter 9 not only utilizes real historic characters, but is also based on the true story of when I dug up the story of Tenskwatawa to try and scare my family. In the end, everyone played along and we all tried to scare each other.) Thus, I loved the proposition of undertaking this project for Schiffer.

As a Ghostorian for Society of the Haunted, I had a number of great locations and real history at my disposal that I wanted to incorporate. One of the things I've enjoyed doing over the years is breaking down the legends and ghost tales to their roots, digging into the

Introduction

past of the old buildings, and discovering the real stories of the people who lived there. Ghosts were once people, and when I enter a haunted location, I try to respect that fact. This time, however, I would be working in reverse, taking that real history and developing my own stories and legends. Creative history at its finest! Needless to say, this was an extremely fun project.

Along the journey, however, personal matters got in the way and long delayed the release of what was supposed to be a quick, easy, and enjoyable write. It was still very enjoyable, but I had to take long spells off from my research and writing, putting everything to the back burner while life reared its ugly head. Months would go by in which attempting to write anything meaningful was relatively pointless. I still wanted this to be a quality piece of work.

What I've put forth here is not only an interesting cross-section of tales and legends from across the Midwest, but the storytelling styles between a number of the tales are also quite different. "Feeling the Afterlife" was an emotional first-person ride, for example, while "The Inscription of Evil Times" is like trying to solve a mystery while reading through an investigator's case notes. Trying different methods of telling the stories was almost as fun as creating the stories themselves!

It is my hope that while you enjoy the tales as they are told, you will be interested enough to dig deeper into the histories of these locations and learn for yourself of the forgotten lives of people who are now but faded memories. They are all quite fascinating, but while there is a little fiction in this truth, there is also quite a bit of truth within this fiction. It's up to you, dear reader, to figure out which is which.

The Dare

Lakeland Asylum–Anchorage, KY

"We're not asking you to be.
We're just daring you to crawl into
the cave."

Go deeper into the tunnel down the hill from Lakeland Asylum.

"I dare you."
"No way!"

The fire snapped and crackled between the three friends on the dark autumn night, little fingers of flame licking the cool air. Faces bathed in a yellow-orange glow, they had begun telling tales of local legends as the hour waned close to midnight. Camping out in Allan's backyard was a summer Saturday night ritual for the three friends in Anchorage, Kentucky.

They'd grown up together: Allan, Vincent, and Becky, the rat pack of the neighborhood. They were rug rats when they first met, now teenagers and a year away from graduation. The camp outs started when they were about ten years old, after Allan had learned to pitch a tent and catalog birds in the Scouts. Occasionally, other friends would join, but the three cohorts were always the mainstays.

Periodically, a dare would be offered around the circle of the crackling fire. Usually, this involved something mischievous, such as swallowing night crawlers, throwing pebbles at bully Billy Prescott's window and laughing at his duck pajamas when he came to investigate, or turning the garden gnomes backwards in Mrs. Sanderson's yard. Tonight's dare, however, was quite different and was outside the neighborhood.

"Come on, Allan," Becky pushed, her wavy sandalwood hair painted auburn in the firelight. "This is a real dare, something real adventurous. No more of this kid's stuff we've been doing for years."

Vincent, with his buzzed blonde hair chimed, "Come on, bro. You can't really be scared of all the rumors. They're just silly ghost stories."

"I don't know about silly." Allan shrugged. "It seems like more and more these days you see on TV that this stuff is real. What if Lakeland is real, too? I'm not a ghost hunter."

Becky scoffed. "We're not asking you to be. We're just daring you to crawl into the cave."

"But they kept dead bodies there."

The location in question was the old Lakeland Asylum, also known as the Central State Hospital. Originally built in 1873 as a home for juvenile delinquents, the brick castle-like building with twin towers was quickly re-purposed for the treatment of patients with psychological disorders, as other local facilities became overcrowded. While reports of abuse began as early as the 1920s, it was in the 1930s that the facility became more notorious for lobotomies and electroshock therapy. The asylum's population quickly grew—overcrowding to 2,400 at one point, when maximum capacity was 1,600—and a number of the occupants committed were neither insane nor psychotic when they first arrived. Fires and murders at Central State were rampant. The cave down the hill from the hospital had been used as a temporary shelter for deceased bodies coming out of the hospital en route to the mass grave sites. Water flowed from a tunnel at the back of the cave, and where that tunnel led was a mystery.

Becky crossed her arms. "We're not even talking tonight, we're talking tomorrow night. So you have a whole twenty-four hours to figure a way out of it."

"Or," Vincent chimed, "a whole twenty-four hours to spook yourself. Think about it. A real cave where they used to store dead bodies. It's zombie apocalypse time!"

Becky punched Vincent in the arm. "Knock it off. Come on, Allan. Tell me you'll do this."

She stared at the midnight-haired teen intently, piercing him with brilliant hazel eyes.

Allan frowned. "We've known each other since kindergarten, Beck. You're not supposed to bat your eyelashes at me in order to try and get your way."

"Oh no?" she smirked.

She leaned in toward him around the fire, inching close to him. Allan thought for a brief moment that she might surprise kiss him as Becky's lips drew near, but she slugged him in the shoulder instead. Vincent burst out laughing.

"You're in," she said. Allan made a move to protest, but Beck held up a finger. "Nope. Don't go there. You don't get to this time."

Resigned to his plight, Allan returned to roasting marshmallows. He had no fear of caves, really, and he certainly didn't believe in the ghost stories that emanated from the entire location. Sure, what happened there was tragic, but restless souls that still roamed the grounds? Come on. That was kid's stuff, right?

What Allan was more concerned about was getting his friends in trouble for trespassing in the middle of the night. There were after-dark curfew laws in place, and those that went venturing out there on their paranormal investigations had received written permission.

The mischief the three friends caused around the neighborhood was much safer. No matter where they tramped off to for some silly prank, they were within a minute or two run of being back in front of their cozy campfire. Becky's Lakeland dare was completely different. Was this one of the ramifications of getting older?

Allan ate his final marshmallow and curled up in his sleeping bag for a restless night's sleep with visions of the zombie apocalypse.

He hadn't found a way out of it. He thought about playing sick, but knew it would be too obvious. He actually inquired his parents about a trip to his grandmother's house out of town, but a day trip there was not in the plans for that weekend. No organization that he was a part of had an event going on that night. He was trapped having to take up the dare at Lakeland.

Becky was waiting for him on his front porch when he exited his house.

He frowned at her and sighed. "Is Vincent here yet?"

"He should be along any moment." Becky frowned back at him. "Gee, don't look so glum. It's all in good fun."

Allan shrugged. "I just have a bad feeling about it."

"Bad feeling, huh? Did you come down with a case of woman's intuition?"

"Isn't something like that your department?"

Becky playfully punched him in the arm. "Really?"

He looked down at where her fist had met his skin. "Do you know how many bruises you've given me over the years?"

"Apparently, not enough."

Allan rolled his eyes as Vincent ambled up the driveway. "Hey, hey! Are we all ready to go?"

Becky turned to their blonde friend. "Did you bring your flashlight?"

"Sure did! Did you bring that audio recorder you were talking about?"

Beck held up a small rectangular black box with buttons. "Absolutely."

Allan didn't like what he heard and crossed his arms. If Becky had in mind what he thought she did, Allan wasn't going to be happy one bit.

"What's that for, Beck?"

A wicked smile melted across her face. "We're just going to do a little ghost hunting, buddy!"

He knew it. She'd been watching too many of those shows on television about teams of so-called paranormal investigators venturing out to locations that were supposedly haunted and trying to catch a ghost. He thought the idea of sitting around and calling out into the ether for some invisible entity to respond was absolutely silly.

He shook his head. "Give me a break, Becky. It's bad enough that you're dragging me to this place to begin with, but now you want me to look like an idiot trying to talk to ghosts? I'm not doing it."

Becky put her hands on her hips. "Yes, you are. There's nothing to be scared of, and it's not like anyone is going to see you other than us. We'll be in a cave—unless you think the ghosts are going to start spreading rumors about you. Maybe they'll tell that pretty Madison Carmichael all about it!"

Vincent chuckled from behind Becky and Allan shot him a nasty look. "So you're in on this, too, are you?"

"Don't worry, Al. If there's a big, bad ghost in that cave, I'll protect you."

Vincent and Becky laughed all the way to the park.

A damp chill permeated the air around them as they passed through the cave entrance. Not understanding where they were headed, they had passed the path they needed to take, accidentally trekking past the small lake and up the hill to where the hospital had once stood. The structure was buried now, in a mound under the earth with piles of dirt covered over the top and simple plant life having grown up over it since. Once they realized they'd missed their turn, they ventured back down, hesitant of the lake in which other stories abounded, including dead bodies that had once floated in the water, and suicides. They adhered to the path until they finally found the small opening in the canopy of trees and plunged in. Fortunately, the cave was only a couple hundred feet into the woods, but it was just a stone's throw from the water's edge of the lake.

They were surprised to discover that the cave entrance was man-made. In fact, most of the cut into the hill had been constructed of stone, brick, and mortar, no more than about fifteen feet wide and not even seven feet tall. Rocks were strewn about the floor, along with a small amount of litter, and the ceiling was calcified over and damp. Along the left side of the cave was a narrow trough built of brick that ran about thirty feet to the rear cave wall, where it met with the square opening of a tunnel no more than a yard wide. Within this trough was a shallow creek of water that ran out of the opening. Discovering where the tunnel led was Allan's dare to fulfill.

Vincent shone his flashlight into the tunnel and peered in. "I don't know, guys. I can't see where this goes. Are you sure about this Becky?"

"Of course I'm sure. He'll be fine, but let's start with the audio recorder first."

"You and your shows," Allan snorted.

"Knock if off." Becky slid the device out of her pocket, flipped a switch on the side of it, and pressed a button. It beeped and she said, "Now be quiet. This thing is actually recording now. Let's see if we get anything."

Allan remained the disgruntled skeptic. "Anything of what?"

Vincent chuckled at his friend. "Of what's going to get you in that tunnel."

"Shh!" Becky scowled at both the boys, then stepped toward the trough of water. "Is there anybody here with us tonight, any spirit that might want to communicate with us? Do you have a name?"

Vincent continued his chucking. "Yeah, Casper."

"Cut it out, Vin." This time it was Allan defending Becky. Even though he wasn't on board with what she was trying to do, he at least figured if they just let her do her thing, they'd be out of that creepy cave much quicker.

Becky continued, "Can you tell us what you did here? How about what you're doing here now?"

The boys finally remained quiet as their friend continued the questioning over the next two minutes, with a ten-second gap between each question to give whatever may have been there a chance to respond. Finally, when Becky was through peppering the air with questions she stopped the recording and hit the play button.

"What are you doing now?" Allan asked.

"I'm going to listen through and see if anything responded." She held the device near her ear as she listened to her own recorded voice rattle off the questions she had just asked. Her face lit up after the question, "Where are you?"

"What was it?" Allan hadn't heard what made Becky get excited, but he was intrigued at the possibility.

"Here, guys. Listen to this." She motioned for the two of them to come close and placed the recorder between them at ear level. "Tell me what you think you hear."

When the section finished playing both Allan and Vincent stared at each other in astonishment. "Did you hear?" they both chimed.

Allan shook his head. "I heard 'go deep.'"

"So did I," Vincent agreed.

"Yup!" Becky was quite pleased with herself and skipped over to the tunnel entrance. "I bet it wants us to go inside. Let's find out!"

Becky began another session with the audio recorder and when they listened to the results again; all three thought they distinctly heard a male voice say, "Deeper."

Becky was ecstatic. "It definitely wants us to go inside. Time to own up to that dare, Allan!"

The teenager shook his head. "Really, Becky? Not only does it have water running through it, but you want me to go into a place where some creepy disembodied voice told us to go into?"

"Yeah! Doesn't that sound fun?"

"It sounds crazy!"

Vincent took a step back. "Yeah, Beck, I don't know about this one."

"Pfft!" Becky grabbed Allan by the hand and pulled him toward the tunnel. "Come on! I'll go with you."

Allan sighed and hung his head. He knew he wasn't going to convince Becky to change her mind. She was the one who really wanted to go exploring in the cave. He had absolutely no desire to crawl though a confined wet tunnel, but he wasn't going to let her go at it on her own either.

"Fine. Let's get this over with."

Vincent took another step backward. "Um, if you two don't mind, I'm going to stand guard out here."

Becky didn't even look back at him as she climbed up the side of the trough. "Yeah, you do that, Vin."

Allan followed her up, but was the first to breach the tunnel entrance. He crawled in, body spread wide, hands and knees on either side of the water that flowed beneath him. He slid a flashlight out from his pocket and shone it up the tunnel. He couldn't see the end.

"Come on, what's taking you so long?" Becky called from behind.

"Yeah, yeah. I'm going."

Grudgingly, Allan crawled up the tunnel, wavering flashlight in hand. It was a slippery trek and he almost fell into the water with nearly every push forward he made. Becky was close behind, impatient, as he carefully plodded up the cold tunnel.

"Can you see the end?"

"What end? It just keeps going. How far have we gone?"

Becky panted. "I don't know. I can't see the beginning of the tunnel anymore. There's just a bit of a glow from Vincent's flashlight. I'm coming up there."

"What?" Was she crazy? "There's not enough room here for both of us."

"Oh, just push to one side and I'll crawl up the other. I want to see how deep this goes."

Allan pressed as much as he could to the left side of the tunnel and huffed. "I'm telling you, it just keeps going, but it's sloping upward a bit, so I can't see the end."

"Oh!"

Becky slipped and screamed, splashing cold water at Allan and shocking his midsection. He reached for her flailing arms and tried helping her out of the trough, but he slipped in as well.

"Crap, that's cold!"

They each scrambled to their respective sides of the tunnel, panting from the water that had stabbed them like ice picks. Allan nearly dropped his flashlight, fumbling with it between his fingers, but was able to secure it just in time. He reached for Becky and made sure she was stable.

"Are you okay, Beck?"

She chuckled. "Yeah, you?"

"Almost dropped the flashlight, but I'm good."

"So, we're finally alone."

Allan was dumbstruck at the comment. It was not only out of place for the moment, but out of place for the friendship they'd cultivated for more than a decade.

"Um, what do you mean?"

"Wherever we go, Vinny is always around."

The wheels were grinding in Allan's mind. He could have sworn her tone and words were of someone who was about to come on to him, but he didn't want to believe it. Admittedly, he had always liked her, but they had only ever been friends. "Yeah, so?"

"Allan, look at me and stop seeing me as the little girl who used to flatten you on the playground."

He obeyed and gazed into her eyes in the pale light of the flashlight and saw her for the first time as a young woman. Hair tousled and wet from the trek through the tunnel, he finally recognized what she meant. "I, uh..."

"There's a reason I always flattened you, why I was always chasing you."

She leaned in and kissed him, and he kissed back. At first, Allan thought it was going to be awkward, but it actually felt quite natural and they lingered there for some time. He wasn't sure how long they'd been kissing when he realized something suddenly felt very wrong. The water was rising. Becky noticed it, too, and broke off.

Allan shone the flashlight up the tunnel. "What's going on?"

"I don't know, but Vin's light has gone out."

"What?"

"Look! There's no light from the end of the tunnel like there had been."

They scrambled back down the tunnel feet first as the water continued to rise. It was up over the sides of the trough and the fronts of their bodies were both thoroughly soaked. What they discovered at the tunnel entrance shocked them both.

"It's blocked!" Allan exclaimed, and he started kicking at a wall of stone and brick while Becky screamed.

"Vincent!"

The water was deeper here than further up the tunnel, and it was backing up quickly. With each kick Allan was splashing icy water into their faces. The blockage wasn't giving way and the terrifying proposition crossed their minds that they might have to crawl back up the tunnel where they had no idea if there was an exit. They very well could be the latest corpses added to the cave.

Finally, the stone started to break free and some of the water started to drain. Both kicked frantically at the blockage and it finally broke open wide with a loud crash of water and rock. They scrambled out of the tunnel and fell to the rock hard floor,

spluttering from the cold water.

"Vincent?" The cave was black as pitch and Allan realized he had dropped the flashlight somewhere back up the tunnel.

A bright light burst on next to them.

"You made it."

Vincent towered next to the two shivering on the floor, and scowled. "I knew what you two were up to."

Becky slapped the blonde teen on the thigh as she tried to rise. "You could have killed us, you idiot!"

"Oh, please. I was just giving you guys a good scare. If you're really going to sneak off on me like that to make out for the first time, you may as well have something to remember it by. I really thought it would have been me, though."

Allan rose to his feet and wiped his wet face. "Vinny, you've been like a brother to me," he sighed and punched him dead in the face.

Vincent staggered backward with a split lip and a loud cackle emanated throughout the cave. He wiped his bleeding mouth and spat. "Yeah, it was a good sucker-punch, Al, but you don't have to laugh about it."

Allan helped Becky to her feet and replied, "That wasn't me."

A low rumble filled the cave. The three friends exchanged nervous glances as the rumble grew in strength until a loud growl burst forth from the tunnel. The shock of the growl overwhelmed the trio and they stumbled over each other bolting out of the cave.

Vincent passed on the next camp-out, which was just as well. Allan and Becky were still none too pleased with the stunt their friend had pulled. It was just as well, as the alone time gave them a chance to explore their budding romance.

After one lengthy kiss in the firelight, Allan asked, "Was that you somehow saying 'go deep' and 'deeper' on those audio clips?"

Becky shook her head. "No. They were real, but very convenient in getting you to go up the tunnel with me."

"Well, even with all that crap that Vincent pulled, I'm glad I went up there with you."

"So am I."

Suddenly, a surge of icy cold water smothered out the campfire and soaked them both. Becky and Allan glanced at each other, then called out into the night, "Vincent!"

The response they received was unexpected and not Vincent's voice.

"Deeper!"

Frigid water welled up around them and they frantically tried to get away, but they were somehow back in the tunnel fighting for their lives, crawling up toward the unknown with only a spectral voice beckoning them forward.

Feeling the Afterlife

Fort Chaffee, AR

I want to scream, to yell out for help, for someone to come and end the agony. At least I can feel again, but something is wrong... very, very wrong.

The Fort Chaffee Field Hospital, abandoned and desolate.

We were on maneuvers in the dead of the night in some godforsaken place. It was an open range, desolate, with small pit craters surrounding us from exercises in the past. You could always hear that faint whistle of the incoming shell before it slammed into the ground and exploded in a ball of fire, illuminating the trees that surrounded what became our ground zero. One time, though, that whistle came too close.

Where have I been? Memories have been somewhat illusive, fading in and out like an old light bulb, but they keep coming. Oh, I've been at Fort Chaffee in Arkansas. That's right. When I first arrived, they showed us the chair Elvis sat in to get his first military haircut back in 1958. The memory seems like it's trapped in a heavy bank of fog, like something out of a dream.

They poke and prod me. I'm not aware of much around, but I hear someone say "critical" and another say that "chances are slim." Do they not know that I can hear them?

I'm right here, fellas! I'm awake!

I can't feel the lower half of my body. I try to move, but I'm completely paralyzed—not my legs, not my arms—nothing. And I can't open my eyes. All is dark except for a red, hazy glow in my periphery.

I vaguely sense that something is jammed up my nose while something else protrudes from my mouth. I don't want to imagine what I look like.

The labyrinth of long interconnecting haunted hallways.

Feet shuffle about the room and low, murmured voices continue to whisper around me. I can't hear exactly what they're saying anymore, but I know it's about me. Their tones are grave and concerned.

There's more poking and prodding while the erratic beat of the heart monitor pulsates in my ear over and over again. Metal clinks and chimes, a man mutters something indiscernible, and an intense pressure presses down on my chest.

This is what it feels like to be a patient.

The room is lucid, almost transparent, yet dark. Is this a dream? A scorching pain in my chest makes it feel like I'm breathing in razors, each inhale labored and difficult. My heart is pounding, rapid and painful. I want to scream, to yell out for help, for someone to come and end the agony. At least I can feel again, but something is wrong... very, very wrong.

The darkness creeps in around me like a suffocating coffin.

My body is tossed onto a roller coaster, convulsing up and down. Oddly, I don't actually lift from the bed with the waves; I experience only the sensation of the ride bounding through what's left of my shredded musculature. The waves get bigger and deeper, my breathing more raspy and painful, and I am helpless to stop it. For a split second, an electric tingle emanates through me and thin, broken streaks of lightning carve crooked paths though the darkness, then disappear. The rippling ride ends, but the journey isn't over. I drift upward, weightlessly rising toward the ceiling.

I can finally see again, but my eyes aren't pained from the sudden introduction of light into my world. In fact, it's not as if I opened my eyelids at all. It's as if a veil or a shroud has been lifted from me, and not only has my sight been restored, but all the pain is gone as well.

The ascent toward the top of the room slows and I hover in midair. What am I doing up here? I turn and gaze down at the thin, pale, destroyed figure of my bloodied corpse.

This is what it feels like to die.

I'm still here, but I'm not. People pass me by, but they don't see me. I try to talk to them, but they don't hear me. The entire complex is bustling with activity, hospital personnel coming and going, but I'm not a part of it. I roam the wards, searching for anyone who will acknowledge me, but no one does.

The halls are all interconnected like one massive labyrinth. I can vaguely remember being informed that the Fort Chaffee Field Hospital was like its own little community, but I had never visited it. I wonder who told me that? Now, it's my home.

Families come to watch movies at the theater, while criminals are hauled into the modest prison section. Soldiers and doctors kick back with a few games of bowling at the small alley, while medications are administered in the psychiatric ward. Sometimes I take a curious glance at what's tossed into the incinerator— usually trash, but sometimes a body part or two. The staff tossing it doesn't seem to mind one way or the other.

And they all remain oblivious to my presence.

What will it take? How can I make myself known? I've longed for that human interaction, for I don't know how many years now. How long has it been? Time feels… different now somehow.

Someone has to know I exist.

This is what it feels like to wander.

Where has everyone gone? This complex had once been so busy with patients, doctors, military personnel of all kinds. Now, they've vanished and the dust continues to collect. These days it's quiet here in a type of eeriness that would make my skin crawl if I still had any. The hallways are long and empty and void of any human life.

The raccoons break in and nest. I try to shoo them off, and sometimes it seems like I do. Perhaps the animals see me sometimes, whereas the humans never did.

I miss them, even though they never knew I was there. Some of them became like friends to me as I followed them about and I learned about their lives. I would perch myself on a counter top and listen to Suzy's or Nancy's or Buddy's stories. Now the only perching that's done at the hospital is by the birds in the rotting rafters.

I hover in the hallways, waiting, listening to the silence.

This is what it feels like to be abandoned.

This is like living a second life. They come in the dead of the night and call for me, wondering if I'm there. Dressed all in black, they carry flashlights, small cameras, and other electronic gadgets that I've never seen before. They claim they can record my voice and listen to it later if I just speak. I call out to them, screaming sometimes, but they don't seem to react at all, except to ask more questions. These new questions don't always correlate with what I just answered, so I get annoyed and throw a piece of moldering plaster down the hallway.

This excites them, and they cry out as if they've seen me. "Did you see that shadow?"

I'm quite more than a shadow! I'm a soldier, fellas!

I run down the hall and they hear my footsteps. Their flashlights bob behind me as they try to catch up. The flash bulbs of the cameras dazzle the decrepit corridors, and I duck into a nearby room. I wonder if they can guess which one. It's like I'm playing hide-and-go-seek again as a child.

Do I remember childhood?

They creep toward me, asking more questions and claiming to see more shadows. One of the raccoons makes a thump in an adjacent ward and the whole gang is startled.

"It must have gone in there!"

Thank you, Mr. Raccoon.

As they inch into the ward I sneak up behind them, floating carefully until I'm directly behind the girl with dark, curly hair. She stops dead in her tracks.

"Guys, my backside is freezing cold and it's like all the hair is standing up on the back of my neck."

They turn around to see her shivering, and I reach over to turn off her flashlight.

Their shrill gives me a bit of a laugh, and I smile. I sort of have friends again.

This is what it feels like on my side of the ghost hunt.

Who are these guys? They look like the same type of people who have been coming from time to time to try and take my picture and record my voice, but the cameras these guys are hauling are much bigger and can be mounted on their shoulders. One guy's hair looks like a black shark fin has been plastered to his head.

It's sweltering hot outside—even I don't like it—but they bear through it with their boisterous gait about the hospital complex. Every room seems to be like a big deal to them, as if the old OB-GYN clinic is going to be the lead story on the evening news. I

shake my invisible head and chuckle. Admittedly, it's entertaining.

I think I'm on TV.

I toy with them a little bit and give the boys a playful show. I lock the bald guy who likes to say "whoa!" in one of the cells until he has to kick the door open really hard with his massive boot. They don't hear me, but I laugh hard all the way down the hall.

This is what it feels like to have fun again.

It's an inferno. Scorching hot heat breathes its volcanic life into me, waves of flames cascading through the dry timber of the complex. The whole thing goes up in seconds in the arid heat of August's roast, buildings torched to the ground like kindling.

The roar of the fire is like a lion's rage—rapid, overpowering, and loud—and I don't know where to run. Every square inch of what I've been calling home for years is consumed in blazing flame. Even in my ethereal state I can feel the searing heat on my body. It tears through me like a tornado of molten lava, and takes with it every last building of what had been the Fort Chaffee Field Hospital.

I try to scream, but billowing clouds of acrid smoke pour out into the night sky, choking off the land—and me. It's all gone.

This is what it feels like to burn and die a second death.

Firemen sift through the ash,

Wasteland, after the inferno of the old hospital.

looking for any remains other than mine. But they're not really looking for me, are they? My body is long since gone, buried in a nondescript grave a few miles away. They're searching for what started the blaze, but even I don't know what caused it and I was here when it started. There will never be a real answer.

Gone are the people with the cameras and gadgets with the lights and those little black devices they said could record my voice. Gone is anyone interested in knowing if I am really here. Gone is my second life.

What had been my home is now a wasteland. Piles of ash and small concrete pillars dot the landscape of the smoldering wreckage.

The firemen leave and I am utterly alone, the silence more prescient than ever. Even the raccoons and birds have fled to make new homes elsewhere. But here I remain, because there is no other place for me to go, after all.

This is what it feels like to linger.

Will I feel anything next?

Silent Killer

Tenkiller Lake, OK

"You said you heard screams
and came to check on the lake?"

Tenkiller Lake. Cool, lucid water laps at the shore of this summer weekend getaway spot. Families, college students, and the like are frequent visitors, enjoying the water for its excellent fishing and recreational swimming. For all the fun times, however, there are the local legends of the lake to respect. Warnings must be listened to, and sometimes the carefree vacationers need to be reminded their enjoyment is something that's given from the lake, not something that's taken from it.

"Come on, bro! It's getting late! There won't be enough light to swim."

"Chill out, Kyle. You really freaking wedged the cooler into the back of the trunk."

"Must have shifted on the ride up."

Kyle and Daniel were both students at the University of Oklahoma and had ventured out to the lake one June weekend with their friends Sandra, Sylvia, and Dipper. Kyle was a strapping, tall, sandy-haired young man who was going to school for a business degree—what business he was interested in he hadn't yet figured out—but had his heart on proposing to Sandra, his long-time girlfriend, once they were finished with college. Daniel was more darkly complected, with thick brown hair and hints of strong Native American features from the heritage on his mother's side. Together, they were gathering the last of their belongings from Kyle's worn SUV to take near the lake shore as the afternoon sun waned.

Finally, the cooler popped and Daniel jerked back from the strength of his pull. He muttered under his breath, but hoisted the cooler out of the trunk, closed it, and joined Kyle at his side.

"Maybe I should pack the trunk next time."

"Whatever. I'm just glad we got the tents packed in there. I hear it gets cold here at night."

Daniel chuckled. "Nah, you just want some alone time with Sandra."

"True. True. What about you and Sylvia?"

Daniel slowed his pace. "What about her?"

Kyle peered out from behind his sunglasses at his friend. "Oh, come on. We've all seen how you look at her. What better time than at a gorgeous lake to finally make your move?"

"Seriously?" Daniel shrugged. "You think she likes me?"

"I have no idea, but this is a great time to take a shot."

"Hey! Come on!" Sandra, a bouncy blonde bounded up to Kyle and kissed him on the cheek. She was already down to her pink bikini and ready to jump into the water. "Put that stuff down so we can swim!"

Kyle grinned but remarked, "I need to set it up first, sweetie."

"There'll be time for that later. Come on!"

Sandra yanked her boyfriend by the arm and the contents of his backpack spilled out onto the ground. She dragged him to the water and splashed into the cool, crystal blue liquid.

A tall, lanky young man with shoulder length sandalwood hair and peach fuzz mutton chops stood up from a fire he'd been starting and exclaimed, "Hey! Not cool, bro, not cool at all! You want us to set it all up while you're in there playing around?"

Kyle paid him no mind and continued to follow Sandra into the lake.

"Yeah, that's right," their friend called out. "You run away from me like that. Tremble in fear of Dipper! You don't know that I was just about to wax you with my ninja moves."

Daniel ambled up next to him with the cooler. "Wax him, huh, Dipper? Don't you think he already does that to his chest?"

The two laughed and a young woman with long, curly jet-black hair emerged from the woods to their left. "Hey, is there a bathroom around here?"

Dipper reached into a nearby plastic bag and extracted a roll of toilet paper. "Call of the wild, young one. Find a tree, but if you're really bold, you'll use leaves instead."

"You're so disgusting, Dipper! Why did we bring you?"

Dipper called out as the brunette traipsed back into the woods, "Because you all love me, Sylvia! In the end, you know I'm your best chance of survival out in the wilderness of–" He turned to Daniel, "Dude, where are we?"

"Tenkiller Lake."

He turned back to Sylvia disappearing behind the trees. "Yeah, this killer lake!"

"I don't think she heard you, Dip."

"You should ask her out, bro."

Daniel shook his head, then remarked, "Hey, what's that?"

Kyle and Sandra were far from the shore and pulling themselves up to a fishing platform out a distance from the small beach.

Dipper patted Daniel's back, "That, my friend, is our last vestige of hope should we get stupid and set the forest on fire."

"I don't want to."

Sylvia was idly painting her toe nails a dark crimson in front of her small, bubble tent. Sandra had been grilling her for the past fifteen minutes about considering Daniel as dating material. Sylvia grew weary quickly from the conversation. She'd known that Daniel had an interest in her, but they'd all been friends for so long that she believed romantic possibilities would be too awkward.

"You need to stop using that as an excuse, Sylvia. Look at me and Kyle. We've all been a part of this circle of friends for years and we're together. I think he might even propose soon."

"And I'm happy for you, Sandra. That is so cool that you've been friends like that for so long and you've been able to take it somewhere else. I just don't feel that way about Daniel. He's just so... Daniel."

Sandra chuckled. "What does that mean?"

Sylvia shrugged. "It just means that I don't really find all that much special about him. He's a nice guy and all, but I need someone that I find interesting."

"Daniel's interesting. He's, well, he has that record for the number of chicken wings eaten at Barnyard's."

"Funny, Sandra! Yes, I should marry the guy who ate so many wings with all that spicy sauce and ended up on the toilet for the next two days."

"Oh, please. No one said anything about marriage. Just give him a chance on a date. Maybe just go on a walk with him tonight."

Sylvia huffed and crossed her arms. "Right. A walk on a moonlit night along the lake. If that's not setting me up for more, I don't know what is."

"Oh, stop it. Just give him a chance."

Kyle shouted over from the fire he had started between the small semicircle of tents. "Come on, girls! Let's roast some marshmallows or something."

The music blared a rhythmic mix of R&B and electronica as the five danced around the fire. Their shadows rose into the trees like great swinging monoliths of onyx misplaced in the branches of the forest. The carousing simmered after a time and their laughter fell more subdued as they returned to the fire's edge for more marshmallows.

Daniel glanced across the fire at Sylvia, and she managed a small smile. *Hopeful,* he thought.

"So, you know this place is haunted, right?" Dipper grinned above the fire as he burned a marshmallow. "Seriously. Like people have died out here and no one knows why."

Kyle scoffed. "Come on, Dip, it's a lake. I'm sure there have been accidents."

Dipper shook his head. "No way, man. People have gone missing for days, and when they're found they've been ripped apart. It's the monster of the lake."

Daniel turned to his oddball friend. "Didn't you ask me earlier today where we were at because you didn't know?"

"I was just goofing around then, but I'm like dead serious now, bro."

Sandra laughed. "You're never dead serious, Dipper. That's why we like you so much. You keep us laughing."

Dipper shoved the marshmallow into his mouth and muffled, "It's your funeral."

Sylvia piped, "Tenkiller Lake is a U.S. Army Corp of Engineers lake created by the dam that was built nearby. It was named for the Tenkillers, a Cherokee family that operated a ferry service across the river. The family name apparently came from a Cherokee warrior during the time of 'The Trail of Tears' who was well-respected by the soldiers around Fort Gibson because of the ten notches in his bow."

"My mother's side is Cherokee," Daniel remarked.

Sylvia smiled again and he became more hopeful.

She concluded, "The point is, there's no such thing as monsters."

Sandra interjected, "What if it's not a monster. What if it's a ghost?"

"See! See!" Dipper stabbed another marshmallow with his stick and held it in the air like a sword. "It's all supernatural! Ghosts, monsters, UFOs—maybe what's out there is the ghost of a monster some UFO dropped off."

Ignoring Dipper's comments, Kyle asked his girlfriend, "What do you mean?"

"Well, on campus there are quite a few haunted places and their stories are all really different. There's Ellison Hall, which used to be an infirmary, and the ghost of some boy that got killed while rollerskating is supposed to be there. They say you can hear him skating through the halls, although others say its actually the sounds of the wheels from the hospital gurneys. A paranormal team named Society of the Haunted just recently did an investigation there and they seem to think the hauntings have more to do with the patients on the gurneys. But who really knows, you know? There's also the Cate Center story, where a boy was decapitated in the dumbwaiter and now his spirit haunts the basement there. So I think every place has its share of wild stories."

Kyle draped his arm around Sandra. "That's my girl. She knows everything!"

"Dude, your girl has some serious moxy." Dipper grinned wildly. "I'm going to have to check me out some ghosts when I get back to school."

Daniel turned to Sandra. "That's all interesting, but how does that relate to the monster story?"

Sandra shrugged. "They're all just tales. The legends that are passed down may have originally started with some piece of real truth, maybe even a lot of truth, but over the years they've been changed, modified, and added to so many times, who knows what the original truth of it is."

Dipper was impressed. "Sandra pulling out the big guns, shooting us with a dose of reality!"

"Is it reality?" Sandra poked a stick into the campfire until the tip caught a flame. "Maybe all the stories are true and we just trick ourselves into thinking they can't possibly be or, like I said, maybe just a small grain of it is true. Which is it?"

Daniel had finally received his wish—a bit of alone time with Sylvia. Sure, he could tell she was reluctant about it, but perhaps with a little time off on their own she would see him in a different light. They'd been friends for about two years now, always hanging out with Kyle, Sandra, and Dipper, but the two of them had never really had any meaningful conversations. Daniel was hoping to make that change.

Sylvia, on the other hand, turned her head and rolled her eyes when Daniel asked her for a moonlit walk along the shore. Sure, he was a friend and they all laughed and had a good time when the gang was out together, but she'd never thought of him as anything more than that. She supposed it seemed natural that with Kyle and Sandra such a heavy couple that she and Daniel should give dating a try as well. Lord knows she wasn't going to date Dipper.

"Beautiful night, don't you think?" Daniel beamed at Sylvia, hoping the smile would convey a message that he was happy to be in her company

Sylvia thought it was a bit much and resisted the urge to roll eyes again. "Yes, it's quite nice."

"Yeah, you've got the moon and the water —" Daniel swallowed hard. "There's you."

The words were suspended in the air between them for a long, awkward moment.

"Daniel, we need to talk about this." Sylvia stared straight ahead as they walked and talked. She was going to let him down and she didn't want to see the pain on his face. They had been friends for a long time, after all, and she still wanted that friendship and the group camaraderie. "You've been a really great guy and friend for a long time now. We all have fun together and a good time hanging out. I don't want to ruin what we have as friends with a relationship when, really, I don't feel like there's a relationship to be had between you and I. So, if we dated for a couple months and it went nowhere, like I think would be the case, and we broke up, then it would be really awkward for all of us to keep hanging out and having fun like we've had. Daniel?"

Daniel was gone. Sylvia spun about in the darkness of the woods, suddenly realizing she was alone. Where could he have gone off to so quickly? Just a moment ago, he had been walking right next to her, and she hadn't heard him dart off into the forest. Was he really that sneaky and just trying to scare her?

"Daniel, come on! This isn't funny." Transfixed, Sylvia stood and listened, but all she heard were crickets. The darkness of Tenkiller's tree cover pressed in on her, the lake's water lapping at the shore's edge nearby. "Daniel!"

Kyle and Sandra were nestled together in a blanket on the fishing platform out in the lake. Kyle had discovered a small canoe near their camp and commandeered it to pack a few things like the blanket and a picnic basket, so he and his girlfriend could enjoy some alone time together out on the lake.

"Do you think they'll hit it off?" Kyle prodded.

"Daniel and Sylvia? I don't think so. Sylvia just really isn't interested in him like that. She's just being nice and is going on the walk with him."

"Ah, that's too bad."

"Well, it's not like we all have to date each other. Hey, do you hear that?"

"Hear what?"

"It sounds like someone is screaming in the distance."

Kyle strained his ears and finally heard it. "Yeah, I do. Is that Sylvia?"

"Oh, no."

Kyle crept to the edge of the platform and leaned over as far as he could to try and hear better. He could tell she was screaming, "Daniel," but it wasn't the type of scream one would make if being attacked, although there was panic.

Sandra shot up from the blanket. "What's wrong with Daniel?"

"I don't know. I'm trying to hear. I think she might be lost. She's saying, 'Where are you?'"

"If he's playing a prank on her, that's one sick joke way out here."

The two strained to hear what their friend was screaming way back near the shore. It was more of the same, "Daniel, where are you?"

"No." Kyle shook his head as he stretched farther out from the platform. "It sounds like they got separated during their walk together."

"But why isn't he responding? He's scaring her!"

"I don't know."

Sandra felt helpless. Far out on the fishing platform, she was unable to do anything to go to the aid of her longtime friend. And to think she had, at one point, encouraged Sylvia to give Daniel a shot at dating! She began calling out into the darkness, "Sylvia! Daniel!"

Nothing. All was silent.

Sandra turned to look at her boyfriend. "What could be—Kyle?"

Kyle was gone.

"Kyle!"

Sandra spun about on the platform, frantically searching for any sign of the young man who had just been sitting next to her as she called out into the night. He didn't dive in; there had been no splash. The small canoe was still moored to the platform, and he wasn't in it. Was this some twisted prank the boys had conjured up to scare the girls?

"Kyle? Kyle! Where are you?"

Sandra realized she was now asking the same question of Kyle as Sylvia was of Daniel.

The lanky, wild-haired young man stirred in the warm confines of his sleeping bag. Vivid images of death devoured his mind, a sea of chaotic flashes cascading across the shore of dreamscape. A large mass erupted from the motley waters, a molten gray of blubbery flesh, towering above the miniscule campsite. It stretched out with one giant multi-fingered hand, its tentacles like massive snakes striking out at its prey. An enormous mouth emerged from its base, bearing razor sharp teeth and unleashing a vicious howl as it lunged for the shore.

Dipper shot straight upright out of his slumber, panting hard. His eyes darted about the darkened tent, but it was his ears that pricked up at the distress. He scrambled to his feet and stumbled out of the tent into the cold night air. Screams pelted him as he spun about and tried to orient himself, the sound of waves enveloping him, but not a ripple on the lake. The lake.

He peered out to where he knew the fishing platform rested, where he knew Kyle and Sandra had ventured out for a romantic moonlit evening. It seemed everyone was hooking up but him: Kyle and Sandra, Daniel and Sylvia—even though he knew Sylvia was more interested in Scott Landon, with the way her eyes lit up anytime he saw the two talking back on campus. That left him alone, but that was cool with him, dude, because everyone would remember him as the life of the party. But where was the party tonight?

In the pale light of the moon he spotted the canoe casting itself away from the platform. Sandra was in it, screaming for Kyle, but Kyle was nowhere to be seen. Sandra frantically paddled, but Dipper couldn't figure out what had spooked her so badly. Was Kyle playing some sort of practical joke on his girlfriend? If so, why wasn't he in on it? Everyone always came to him with the practical jokes.

Another scream permeated the air to his left and Sylvia darted out of the woods and into the center of the campsite. She yanked Dipper's arm and tried to pull him back from where she came.

"Whoa! What the hell is going on, Sylvia?"

"It's Daniel! Daniel is gone, just vanished. At first I thought he was playing a joke, but he's been trying to pick me up all night. He wouldn't just abandon me like that. And now I think I hear Sandra screaming."

Dipper pointed out to the lake. "Yeah, she's paddling back in the canoe, but like Kyle isn't with her. What the –?"

Sylvia stared out at the water. "What are you talking about? There's no one there."

It was true. Where Sandra had just been moments ago, paddling frantically, there was now nothing. The water was placid, with barely a ripple, as if nothing had ever been at all. All was silent.

Dipper scooped his jaw from the ground and stammered, "I—I don't get it. She was just there!"

"Are you sure? Maybe she's back on the platform with Kyle and you're just not seeing them."

"She was screaming for Kyle; didn't you hear her? And I'm telling you she was out in the canoe." Dipper cupped his hands to his mouth. "Sandra! Kyle!"

Sylvia joined him in yelling across the lake. "Kyle! Sandra! This isn't funny, guys! Daniel!"

The cool waters of the lake gently caressed the shore, but were otherwise still as death. The pale moonlight, instead of a reflective shimmer on the water, seemed to be absorbed into the lake itself, its light diffused by the murky depths.

Sylvia pointed off to the right. "What's that?"

Dipper squinted at first, then his eyes bulged in recognition of the object that was gliding across the water. "It's the canoe!"

They rushed to the water's edge and followed it south to a section of shoreline where it seemed the canoe might land. No one was visible inside.

"Sandra!" Sylvia screamed out in the canoe's direction, but there was no response.

The two paced up and down the small section of shore as the canoe slowly drifted toward them. Aimlessly it floated across the water, yet it seemed destined to arrive right at their feet.

Dipper suddenly perked up, a prickly rush coursing through his veins. "Wait. Isn't this where Kyle first found the canoe? Like right in this very spot?"

Sylvia shook her head. "I really don't know. Daniel was too busy trying to talk me into walking with him."

"It's just too weird, man."

"Very odd, indeed." The gravelly voice echoed from behind them.

Dipper and Sylvia spun about to face the owner of the voice they did not recognize and discovered before them the diminutive figure of an elderly man. His face was tan, harsh, and weather-beaten, his long, white hair pulled back in a pony tail, and his dark eyes lacked emotion.

Dipper swallowed hard. "Who are you, dude? Where did you come from?"

The old man was slow to answer. "I'm the keeper of the canoe. It shouldn't have been touched."

Sylvia cowered next to Dipper and shouted, "What have you done with our friends?"

The old man spread his rough hands. "I've done nothing. I heard the screams and came to check on the lake."

The two friends were disconcerted and alarmed at the words the old man had chosen—that he had come to check on the lake and not the source of the screams. The canoe finally washed up to the shore behind Dipper and Sylvia and they peered inside. No one was in the canoe.

"Lose something?"

The most unlikely couple of the small band of friends held tight to each other as the old man's words haunted them.

Sylvia replied, "You said you heard screams and came to check on the lake?"

"Yes. The lake."

Dipper stepped back toward the water's edge, taking Sylvia with him. "Dude, you're creeping me out."

"Not to worry. I won't for—well, that didn't take very long."

The old man turned and walked away from the lake. Where Dipper and Sylvia once stood was now devoid of anyone. They had completely vanished.

Five friends disappeared into the cool night at Oklahoma's Tenkiller Lake without a trace. Local law enforcement found their campsite and vehicles completely undisturbed, as if they had just walked off into the forest and melted into the landscape. The only other object of note nearby was a small canoe resting silently nearby at the edge of the lake. It's keeper was unknown, but known by all that listened to the legends of the lake.

The Last Laugh

Villisca, IA

...gouge marks from the upswing of the ax were discovered in the ceilings of the upstairs bedrooms, and the bloody ax was found in the room with the Stillinger girls.

Thousands of visitors had preceded her over the decades. From near and far they came to view the spectacle, to engross themselves in the mystery, to see if something would send them into a panic and scare them off the property. The spectacle was what has come to be known as the Villisca Ax Murder House, the mystery was one that had been unsolved for over 100 years, and the scare was of the restless spirits that still reside in the old farmhouse.

To say Kasey was nervous stepping into the house was an absurd understatement. She'd heard plenty of the tales of visitors being pushed and pulled around the house by something unseen, and the television shows that had featured the hauntings of the old home only intensified her fear. A bead of sweat dripping down her brow met her first step across the threshold in unison.

The story was infamous for the small Iowa town of Villisca. On a sleepy June night in 1912, two adults and six children were brutally murdered with an ax while sleeping in their beds. Josiah B. Moore, his wife, Sarah, their children Herman, Katherine, Boyd, and Paul, and two local girls who were sleeping over, Lena and Ina Stillinger, had their lives stolen from them in the middle of the night by an unknown assailant. All the curtains had been drawn, the bodies had been covered with bedclothes after they were murdered, kerosene lamps were found at the foot of the beds of J.B. and Sarah Moore and the Stillinger girls, a pan of bloody water and a plate of uneaten food had been found in the kitchen, gouge marks from the upswing of the ax were discovered in the ceilings of the upstairs bedrooms, and the bloody ax was found in the room with the Stillinger girls.

Of all the victims, only 12-year-old Lena Stillinger appeared to have attempted to fend off her attacker with a defensive wound on her arm. But there was a blood stain on the inside of her right knee and she was wearing no undergarments, suggesting something more sinister.

There had been no shortage of suspects, which included an Iowa State Senator who lived in town, a traveling preacher whose trial was considered a mockery and resulted in a hung jury, a prominent serial killer, a man accused of killing his own family in the same manner as the Moore's, and an assortment of hobos and transients. There were even others who attempted to admit to the murders on their death beds, but the facts within their confessions didn't line up with the true facts of the case. To this day, the murders remain unsolved and likely forever will be.

Now Kasey stiffened inside that same chamber of horrors with her friend, Allison— alone together. Why couldn't Robert have come? He was well-versed in both history and the paranormal, but when she had asked him, he had already made other plans for that night. She called him just before arriving, and they discussed the home's dark past and the experiences of those who have entered since. He'd been part of a group that witnessed a ghostly little girl hiding under one of the beds upstairs. Nothing sinister had happened to them, he assured Kasey.

Kasey couldn't be as sure as he. A rush of ice-cold blood seared through her veins, and her eyes darted to the door. Immediately, she was dizzy.

Allison grabbed her friend's arm. "Don't get spooked on me already! We have all night in here."

All night. Kasey couldn't believe she had signed up for this, but it was Allison's birthday wish, so here they were putting their souls in jeopardy. Why couldn't Allison have wanted to go to a club or something for her birthday?

Kasey sighed. "I'm fine. This is what you wanted, so let's do this. It's just a house."

"Think we'll run into the murderer? They say his spirit is here, too."

"I know, hiding in the attic, but some have encountered him in the basement. Let's just stay away from those two spots?"

Allison shook her head and laughed. "Are you kidding?"

Almost as if in response, Kasey swore she heard children laughing. "Did you hear that?"

"Hear what?"

It was the last laugh Kasey would hear.

She awoke in complete darkness. Kasey's eyes shot open, but there was nothing to take in. Beneath her, the floor was hard and wooden, a sign she may still be in the Villisca house, but where was she?

"Allison?"

No answer. Kasey spun about, arms flailing, groping for some sort of object or surface. Her palms slapped walls within a mere couple feet of her and then a door. She sprung for the door and pulled herself up against it. In the darkness she found the handle, but it didn't budge.

"Allison!"

Again, no answer. Kasey yanked and pulled on the handle, shrilled her friend's name at the top of her lungs, and slammed her shoulder against the slab of wood that blocked her escape.

"No. How is this possible?"

She slammed her shoulder into the door again to no avail. She wanted to cry, but didn't. Trapped in a closet, she presumed. Trapped in a closet in a house where an entire family had been murdered. She stepped back to think for a moment and that's when she felt the chill. Frigid fingers crept across her neck from behind, and a frosty breath blew into her right ear. She stood stock still, hoping it would go away, but it lingered as if someone was directly behind her, tickling her neck.

"Please, just go away."

She felt something warm and wet trickle from her nose. A nose bleed, perhaps, but there was no way for her to tell in the pitch blackness.

Suddenly, the door swung open and Kasey bolted through, crashing to the floor of the small bedroom on the other side. She scrambled to the far wall and bounced up.

"Allison! Thank God you opened that door when you did. Allison?"

Kasey stood alone in the room, a solitary silhouette beside a window frame, her friend nowhere to be found. However, she wasn't quite alone. A little girl lay sleeping in a bed against the adjacent wall, oblivious to the noise Kasey had just created crashing to the floor and calling out into the cool night air.

Kasey took a step toward the girl, tempted to wake her and ask her who she was and what she was doing in the house sleeping in the bed. It would be wrong to disturb the little girl, right? Katherine? And where were the other children?

No time to think. The bedroom door creaked open, and a large, dark figure stepped into the bedroom. He was dressed in blood-splattered overalls and he wielded an ax in his right hand, while he slicked his mangy hair back with his left. His heavy work boots thudded against the floor as he approached the bed, and the little girl startled awake.

The nearby train rattled the entire house.

"Mr. Jones? Reverend Kelly?"

Kasey knew exactly what was about to happen. Had she been pulled back in time to thwart the murder? There was no time to ponder the why of where she was at, she just needed to act. Kasey lunged toward the murderer and screamed.

"Get away! Don't you hurt her!"

But it was too late. He raised the ax as Kasey hurtled toward him and embedded it deep into the innocent little girl.

"No!"

Kasey's vision exploded into crimson. The whole room was soaked in the color of blood as the ax fell again and bludgeoned the young girl. She reached for the murder's arm and missed, her momentum carrying her through the open door and into the short hallway. She spun around to make another run at the figure, but the bedroom door slammed shut in her face.

"No!' Kasey pounded her fists against the door and yanked on the doorknob, but it was locked tight and wouldn't budge. "Leave her alone!"

Kasey grew more light-headed with each blow to the door, and she began to cry. She had just witnessed one of the infamous murders and had been powerless to stop it. She sank to the ground in disbelief, in shock, and in despair.

Perhaps she'd get the bastard on his way out of the bedroom. No. He was too big and he was armed with that ax. She had to get somebody. She needed to run and find a neighbor—find somebody—before he escaped from his repulsive crime again.

Kasey bolted down the stairs and stopped in her tracks at the sight of the two Stillinger girls already murdered in the first floor bedroom. Was she too late for everyone?

Out of place for the horror of the house, the strong odor of bacon wafted through the air and permeated her nostrils. What was the purpose of the bacon? A slab of it had been found lying near the ax in the room with the Stillngers. But right now the murderer was upstairs wielding the ax. No. The ax was there in the room resting against the wall. Kasey didn't understand.

She staggered toward the front door, her mind swirling with fear, sadness, and confusion. She wiped her nose and her own fresh blood smeared across her hand. She didn't care. She had to get out that door and find help. When she reached it the knob gave way to her turn and she opened it.

"Oh, hello, Ms. Moore."

Kasey was dumbstruck. "I'm sorry?"

Two men stood before her, one fair skinned and short in a brown suit with a matching hat and another taller, rougher, with a receding hairline shaved down and wearing faded black work clothes.

"Sarah, you look a fright." The smaller man's face grew grave. "It's me, Reverend Kelly. You don't look well, ma'am."

"I'm sorry. You're who?"

"Reverend Kelly, ma'am. And this is William Mansfield. Do you recollect that we were going to call today for some possible work for William? I'd met him during my travels and he was looking for work. Is your husband home?"

The faces of the men were spinning in her head and Kasey grabbed the door frame to maintain her balance.

The taller of the men spoke in a gruff tone. "You don't look well, ma'am. I reckon she needs some water, Reverend."

The voices melted into the distance as Kasey fell to her knees. Around her a blackness closed in until she grew numb and was no more. She didn't even feel her head smack into the ground.

A faint voice was trying to coax her to consciousness. It sounded familiar, much like Allison, but why were children screaming in the background? The screaming subsided and all that remained was the voice that was trying to comfort her.

"Mom?"

"Oh, Lord, you really did hit your head hard."

Kasey's vision began to clear, but before her was an unfamiliar face, although she recognized she was laying upon a sofa in the living room of the Villisca house. "I'm sorry, you are?"

"Mary, dear. Mary Peckham from next door. Oh my, what is that mark on your neck?" The strange woman felt Kasey's head for a temperature. "You best be well for the Children's Day program tomorrow at the church."

"Children's Day program?"

The strange man that had introduced himself as a Reverend appeared at Mary's side. "I apologize, ma'am, for startling you. William found your husband and even met a couple of your children. He's mighty fond of the little ones and says they even remind him of his own. Looks like this will be a good fit for him for work. Josiah already has him chopping some wood out back."

Mary nodded her head in approval. "Sometimes these things just work out that way with the way the Lord puts people together. Wouldn't you agree, Sarah?"

Kasey looked up, her eyes darting back and forth between Mary and the Reverend. Maybe she wasn't really Kasey. Perhaps she really was Sarah Moore and had just dreamed of a life in the future as a woman named Kasey. Her head began spinning again, her mind a fog, but she managed to reply, "Yes, ma'am. I suppose so."

Paranormal Wine

Belvoir Winery—Liberty, MO

The wine flutes between the two friends shook, ripples expanding in the cool fragrant liquid.

The Belvoir Winery in Liberty, Missouri.

Michael fired up a cigar and handed his friend, Leigh, the bottle of wine.

Leigh spied the bottle curiously. "What's the vintage?"

"A 2008 Norton from Belvoir Winery."

It was wine tasting night, an evening in which the two friends regularly partook every other week. Usually, they sat out on the back veranda of Michael's home and watched the moon rise over the lake behind his house, but summer was laboring into August and the humidity was severe. Weather forecasters were calling for thunderstorms, but what do they ever know? It would probably remain sticky and sultry outside all night. Whatever the case, however, the two friends decided the wine tasting would be better conducted indoors that evening and relaxed in the rear sun room of the home.

"Belvoir Winery? Where's that at? Should I know it?"

Michael popped the cork on the bottle and poured the contents into two wine flutes. "Liberty, Missouri. It's a bit of an unusual location. The facility used to be the old Odd Fellows Home District, which still has a few of the buildings standing. The Administration building is where the winery and a small pub are housed, with a small museum section for the Odd Fellows and a conference area."

Shadows are frequently seen down the halls of the Old Folks home.

"So it's fully functional?"

Michael handed one of the flutes to Leigh. "Oh, definitely. People go up there all the time and there are even ghost tours that are run out of the place. Sounds like the storm is rolling in."

The soft rumble of thunder resounded in the distance and the lights flickered.

"Ghost tours? Really?"

"Absolutely. There are supposed to be a couple ghosts in the admin building where the winery is, but the other couple buildings—the Old Folks Building and the Old Hospital—they're pretty haunted, too."

The lights flickered again.

Leigh sighed. "I hope they don't go out. The storm doesn't even seem to be that close yet. Well, you can't be serious about this ghost business. You don't really believe in all of that, do you?"

"Well, let me tell you, I really didn't at first. However, after getting the tour for myself, I now think differently of the matter."

"You've got to be kidding me."

"Oh, no. I'm quite serious."

The wine flutes between the two friends shook, ripples expanding in the cool fragrant liquid.

Leigh frowned but enjoyed another sip of wine. "The storm must be getting closer. It's shaking our wine."

Michael eyed the glasses. "Yes, but I didn't actually hear the thunder this time."

"Well, you're enamored with telling me you now believe in ghosts, so you probably didn't hear it. So, then tell me, my friend, what exactly do you think you saw at Belvoir Winery?"

"Well, I have to tell you that I think I saw something as soon as I pulled up to the building."

"Oh, come now."

"No, I'm quite serious. I thought I saw someone looking out one of the top windows, but when I mentioned something to the tour guide just before we started, she told me that no one had been upstairs all day."

Leigh rolled his eyes. "Seriously? You want me to believe this?"

Michael spread his hands. "Oh, I know. That's not a very good experience and it certainly didn't sell me on the place being haunted, but it was a nice little teaser to get the night started. Who knows what it may have been."

"So then what exactly happened to make you think the place is haunted?"

Thunder cracked again, shaking the portraits on the walls within their frames. The lights didn't flicker, but grew dim within the sun room.

Leigh spun about. "Brown out?"

"Perhaps." Michael held up his flute. "Did I tell you the wine is very good?"

"I'm sipping some right now. Yes, it's very good."

"Very well then. I'll tell you the tale. It was in the Old Folks home that I became convinced. Oh, we did spend some time in the Old Hospital, which was definitely very creepy. Some of the others I was with claimed to have seen something, but I didn't. However, it did feel very dark and heavy inside, like someone was pressing down on you from behind. There's also a bunker out back behind the buildings that they take you to and, again, others claimed they saw a large shadow moving about, but I didn't. I only saw a mouse scurrying across the floor."

Leigh shrugged. "Scary enough if it had been a rat."

"No, it was just a field mouse. But, like I said, it was really in the Old Folks home that I truly believe I saw something paranormal."

"Ah, there's that term. Paranormal."

The wine flutes between them shook again, and the two friends exchanged perplexed glances.

Michael gazed out the window toward the lake. "I didn't hear thunder that time. In any case, look, I'm serious. Here's what happened. We were on the second floor down some godforsaken hallway—I really couldn't tell you which one—but at the end of the hall there was another corridor. It was within that corridor that I swore I saw someone walking around. I called out to the person, but everyone else in the group told me to be quiet. So I told them, 'Look, there's someone down at the end of the hallway. They probably shouldn't be up here.' One of the guys told me that it was someone that we weren't going to make go away."

"So was it a prowler or are you telling me this was your ghost?"

The lights in the sun room suddenly went out, yet the ones in the rest of the house remained on. A soft rumble in the distance alerted the friends that the weather was moving away from them.

"You know, Leigh, the lights going out in this single room can't be from the storm, especially if it's moving on."

Leigh puffed his cigar, failed to realize it had been extinguished, and raised a finger. "Don't start with me. If you're trying to scare me it won't work. You come back from your trip and try to spook me with ghost stories on a stormy night? Forget it. It's not going to work."

Michael waved him down. "Just listen. So we inched closer and everyone was being really quiet. We could see this person pacing back and forth in that corridor at the end of the hall, but he wouldn't acknowledge us. Just before we got to the end of the hall, the person stopped pacing and remained in the corridor to the right. One of the guides said 'hello' and asked the person his name, but there was no response. Now, I had been standing about in the middle of the pack of a group of about ten and on the right side. I thought no one had been off to my right, but there was suddenly someone there. I couldn't really see him, but I knew it was a male about my size, the form of a man standing there facing me."

Finally intrigued, Leigh leaned in closer to listen to the story. He didn't even care to mention the icy, prickly feeling that was creeping up his back and completely out of season for a humid evening in August. "Who was it?"

"I'm getting to that. I turned to try and whisper something to him, and he got real close, almost right up into my face. The insane part about it all is that I couldn't make out any features about him at all. It was just a black figure no matter how close he got to me. Then he suddenly blew right past me—right through me—and down the corridor on the left side. But this is where it gets even odder. It was like he evaporated right in the middle of the hall! He didn't duck into any rooms, anything. We even checked them all. I just saw his form running down that hall and then it was like he melted into the darkness."

Leigh was finally engrossed in the tale. "That's actually rather amazing. I would never have believed it, if you weren't the one to have told me."

Suddenly, a candle to Leigh's right sprang to life and he jumped out of his seat.

Michael grinned. "Oh, did I forget to mention? He came home with me."

The Albino Lady

North Topeka, KS

"Oh, please, she doesn't scare people." "And she really doesn't have much to laugh at. I grew up around here and her tale was a sad one."

"When and where did you see her?"

It was the question that was to hang in the air all night. Liz Bradley, a local storyteller of North Topeka, Kansas, had organized "Albino Lady Night," a participative story-telling evening in the cemetery in which the area's most famous ghost frequently visited. She had led them by torchlight up a gradual embankment to the top of the small hill in the center of Rochester Cemetery, a location many in the small crowd had never been. Most residents simply drove by the cemetery without taking more than a glance, but few ventured in and even fewer trekked into the heart of the graveyard, where a collection of headstones circled an old, leaf-barren tree.

The torch now rested in a sconce near a tall stone bearing a cross, and Liz addressed the small throng, about twenty in all, that braved the cool chill of the autumn evening. The group was dead silent.

She had already told them about some of the relevant history, that the "Albino Lady," as she'd been known in the area, had at one time been a true local resident of what had been Rochester, a town once filled with the promise of a railroad connection that never materialized. Now the road, school, and cemetery were part of North Topeka, where the Albino Lady had once lived and worked until her death in the mid-1960s. Her skin was a stark white, her wiry hair even whiter, and all recalled her blazing pink eyes, each detail of her real physical description the same as her ghostly one now told in tales about the cemetery and local area.

"Come on. This is supposed to be interactive. No?" Liz shook her head. "All right. I'll go first to break the ice. It was just down the hill from whence we came, and I saw her gliding along the road like an apparition, but not really, since she wasn't translucent. The lady was solid, but her pale skin glowed in the moonlight and made her look ghostly. I tried to follow her, but her walk seemed to be so much quicker than my run and I lost her amongst the headstones near the entrance of the cemetery. There was one other time that I thought I saw her out of the corner of my eye around the same area, but it happened so quickly that I'm not exactly sure if it was her I saw or something else. She's not the only ghost and restless spirit around this cemetery, after all."

Murmurs permeated the crowd and heads nodded in approval. It was a start and Liz knew she'd now get a couple members of the group to open up. Once those couple opened up, the stories would start flowing.

One nervous young woman in a pink hoodie raised a hand.

A smile warmed across Liz's face. "Yes, go ahead, dear."

"Well, I just wanted to say that I think she must have owned a dog because, the one time I saw her, I was here in the cemetery and she just walked across with a big white German Shepherd that also had pink eyes. She didn't say anything and the dog didn't make a sound. It was like they just floated by."

Liz nodded. "The idea that she had a dog isn't uncommon. There have been quite a few reports that her ghost has been seen with the ghost of a dog, too. The type of dog changes, though. Some have said she's walking a poodle, while others have reported her with a pit bull or a German Shepherd."

A bald, middle-aged man in a dark blue windbreaker spoke up. "I think she had a dog, too. I actually spoke with her one time—her ghost, I mean. Again, yeah, it was right here at the cemetery. My buddies and I actually came here to try and find her years ago and we got what we wished for. She came up to us with the dog—I do remember it as a poodle, so go figure—and she wanted to know what we were doing. So we told her that we were actually looking for her, and she told us, 'You boys better get going. I have to leave now.'"

The crowd grew lively with chatter. The idea that the Albino Lady had actually spoken with someone really interested them and a young college girl asked, "Did you record it? Did you have any equipment with you to get what she said on audio? What did her voice sound like?"

The middle-aged man chuckled. "Heh, no. I'm not one of those paranormal investigators, and back in the day, we had no idea that there was even such a thing as ghosthunting. We were just a couple of kids going out the cemetery to find her because we'd heard the stories. I kind of remember her voice as light with a bit of a rasp to it. Really, she didn't sound much different than any other elderly woman I've talked to."

Liz was impressed that the crowd had become interactive with each other and discussions were sprouting around the circle about what people had experienced, rather than she having to prompt every remark. She decided to prod a little further. "Those are some great stories, but they're all about the cemetery here. While the Albino Lady is most commonly seen here, is there anywhere else that someone has seen her?"

"I've seen her walking down the road!" It was a male voice from somewhere in the crowd, but no one laid claim to the comment, although everyone started searching around for the speaker.

"Good, good." Liz wanted more than that. "Which road? Anything else that was going on at the time? Were you driving?"

There was no reply as heads continued to swivel. Random comment. Liz got those sometimes in these settings.

"All right. Well, anyone else with a roadside haunt from the Albino Lady, or anywhere else for that matter?"

"I have one!" The call came from a plus-size blonde in her mid-thirties.

Liz acknowledged her and the woman continued.

"When I saw her, I was just a kid and we saw her down by the river not too far from here. She was on the other side just standing on the bank staring at us and laughing like crazy. Scared us to death!"

Surprised, Liz responded, "I don't hear about too many sightings down by the river. And she was laughing? That's a little different."

"Crazy white hair and pink eyes—yep, that was her. It was like she was trying to scare us away from there for some reason."

"Oh, please, she doesn't scare people." The response came from a diminutive old woman at the back of the crowd wrapped heavily in a shawl. "And she really doesn't have much to laugh at. I grew up around here and her tale was a sad one."

The blonde stood by her story. "I saw what I saw."

"Then maybe you saw something else. There are other spirits around here, after all."

Curious, Liz turned to the old woman. "What tale of hers do you have? If you say she didn't have much to laugh at, do you remember much about her?"

"Oh, I remember her well. She was a very quiet and reserved woman who worked for years as a housekeeper and, for a while, at Duckwall's Store on North Kansas Avenue. It was hard for her to have found employment as much else, and she lived a secluded life in a small house near the cemetery here. There were many stories that made the rounds about her. After all, because of her condition, she really only came out at night, but she enjoyed her strolls through the moonlight. The darkness of the night was quiet like she, and in the pale light she glowed, almost as if she were a living apparition. So it's no wonder she's still seen walking past here on one of her strolls in the afterlife. It's as comfortable to her now as it was then."

"So you've seen her then? Here in the cemetery?"

"But of course. The few friends she had are here, and it's usually quite quiet, the way she likes it—but not tonight."

The old woman turned and walked down the small hill without another word.

"Wait." Liz pushed through the small crowd to catch up to the old woman. "It sounds like you knew her personally. We'd love to hear more."

The others followed, excitedly commenting about the story, but as they rounded the hill the old woman was nowhere to be seen. The excited comments turned to gasps and cries of dismay. With her tale still hanging in the air, the old woman vanished in silvery moonlight as if she had been nothing but an apparition.

The Inscription of Evil Times

Conover, IA

We have fallen upon evil times
and the world has waxed very old
and wicked.
Politics are very corrupt.
Children are no longer respectful
to their parents.

Introduction

For years now I have been defining the term "Ghostorian" as:

One who researches and investigates a ghost and the place in which it haunts.

I, Mike Ricksecker, am a Ghostorian.

This case came to me out of nowhere. A man who called himself Dr. Patrick approached me one fine afternoon and asked me if I would consider researching for him a matter of grave importance. I asked him what he had in mind and he proceeded to unveil documents concerning an ancient tablet with an archaic inscription and an old tattered journal he claimed dated to the 1860s in Iowa.

Dr. Patrick insisted the two historic pieces were related, and it is from those two sources that this investigation began. I did not expect at all for it to take me where it did.

I have opened my case file to present these thirteen exhibits. Make of it what you will.

EXHIBIT 1:
Journal Entry #1

It began in darkness. Elle awoke coughing and then took to the fever. Within just days she was taken from us and we are still in complete shock. We can only assume that the Lord had bigger plans for her, but the children are now without their mother and me without a wife. Life suddenly became much more difficult than it already was and I am without desire. The service was today. Elle's family attended and Reverend Williams presided. I can't say it wasn't a lovely service, but it was preceded with a small mystery. Yesterday, as we took to the task of digging the plot near the cottonwood, we unearthed a stone tablet of sorts. Upon it was carved an inscription unlike any we had ever seen. We removed it from the ground and brought it up to the house so we could continue our labor.

I asked Reverend Williams about the inscription today after the service and showed him the tablet, and he claimed to not know what it meant. Yet it struck me that he may not have been entirely truthful and somewhere in his words was a falsehood. I know I ought not to say that about the Lord's trusted servant, but I believe Reverend Williams does know something of the tablet and its inscription. Why he wouldn't tell me I cannot guess.

I may ask Elle's sister to stay with us a spell. She's a spinster, but a temporary caretaker for the younger children may lend to be helpful.

Dr. Patrick's Note:

While this is not the first encounter with the tablet and the inscription in the chronology, I have presented it first to illustrate the innocent nature in which it seemed acquired. It is also quite suspect that they buried their loved one in the same hole from whence it came.

EXHIBIT 2:
The Inspection

Dr. Patrick's Note:

This is not the first I have seen of this inscription. My original observance was in Istanbul on a tablet in a museum. My published notes on the matter are as follows:

In the museum at Constantinople the writer saw an inscription upon an old stone. It was by King Naram Sin of Chaldea, 3800 years B.C., and it said,

We have fallen upon evil times
and the world has waxed very old and wicked.
Politics are very corrupt.
Children are no longer respectful to their parents.

This old and ever-recurring complaint does not depend upon any actual deterioration of the times, for the times are constantly growing better. It comes usually from older people whose outlook may be biased by subjective conditions due to decaying powers and by the tendency to regard all changes as changes for the worse, the only really good times being the bright days of our own youth.

It is curious that a facsimile of the inscription was found here in America thousands of years after the original was carved. Its provenance is important, but indiscernible at this time. This is a matter more appropriate for my colleagues in archeology, but I am drawn to the mystery of this tale and why it has found me again.

EXHIBIT 3:
Journal Entry #2

Elle's sister has been murdered, stabbed six times with one of the kitchen knives. Reverend Williams called upon the house and offered his blessing. He has called us to prayer to repent, for we have lost the way of the Lord during these dark times. Sin has plagued the home since Elle caught the fever. We've been cursed for our sins. I should never have lied to Rogers about what happened to his horse during that hail storm.

The children are frightened. Young Mary even claimed to the Reverend that she had seen her mother just a fortnight ago, walking the grounds in the moonlight. Blasphemous child, according to Reverend Williams. My family is falling apart. The mayor is interested in the stone tablet that was found at Elle's gravesite. He believes if the interest in the railroad doesn't hold fast, then maybe scholars would be interested in local history. I can't imagine a scholar being interested in this land at all.

Dr. Patrick's Note:

This is the final entry on the final page of the journal. At this time it is unknown whether there is another volume with additional entries concerning the family in question.

EXHIBIT 3B:
Ghostorian's Notes

It is possible that the journal may have been written by Elijah Dobson. He was born in 1833 in Lancaster, Pennsylvania, and married Giselle Pruitt in 1855. Giselle died in 1867 in Conover, Iowa. She was survived by her husband, sons William and Paul, and daughters Martha, Elizabeth, and Mary. She had a sister, Elvira, who died in 1868, also in Conover, Iowa.

Elijah Dobson died in 1881 in Kansas City, Missouri. Census records from 1870 show that the family moved there prior to the 1870 record. Oddly, Mary was not listed on the census record and I can find no record of her death.

Although not unusual for records of that period of time, I can find no cause of death for Giselle, Elvira, or Elijah. The remaining children, save for Elizabeth, scattered across the country. William passed away in Grantsville, Utah, in 1922, Paul in Villisca, Iowa,

in 1913, and Martha as Martha Johnston in Guthrie, Oklahoma, in 1931. Elizabeth never married and passed away in Kansas City in 1943. Although I can find no original record of purchase, the house Elizabeth lived in when she died was still in the name of her father, Elijah, upon her death.

Understandably, there is some room for doubt; these are those closest records I could find to match the journal entries with that time frame in Iowa. Giselle can easily be shortened to Elle; she had a sister who died just a year later, she had a daughter by the name of Mary who was considered young, and there are other children in the picture.
I will continue to look for additional information to support my theory that this is the family in question.

EXHIBIT 4:
An Iowa Ghost Encounter

Ghostorian's Note:

The following was submitted by inquiry via Internet in a request for local folklore near former Conover, Iowa, after discovering a few reports of sightings near Calmar. These consisted of little one-liners such as:

"Along the trail outside of Calmar is an old foundation where an eerie mist forms on nights of the full moon."

"There's the foundation of an old witch's house near Calmar that is haunted by a freezing white mist on some nights, even though it's warm outside."

From ghostmommy1985:

Although it's about 45 minutes away, we had all heard about the haunting along the Prairie Farmer Recreation Trail near Calmer and we wanted to make the trip to check it out. The legend as we've heard it is that if you sit in the center of the foundation of an old farm out near one of the fields, then the temperature will drop about thirty degrees and a white mist will form around the foundation. Moans cry out from the mist and, if you're not careful, then hands will pull at you and drag you into a pit of hell in the middle of the ruins.

Well, that's not exactly how we experienced it, but we did experience something.

We got the location of the foundation from a reluctant local, but we had to explain ourselves pretty thoroughly and Casey bought him a case of beer. Apparently, a lot of teens head out there to party and make out, but we told him we were more interested in finding the remains of the structure and maybe discovering something historical. When he told us of all the

[story continued on following page]

partying out there, we suddenly weren't very hopeful to find much of anything.

Fortunately, we did find what seemed to be an old stone foundation and, just like we'd been told; it was littered with empty beer cans and cold embers from little fires. The three of us hung out for a while taking pictures and just getting a sense of the place, but there really wasn't much. We kicked around the embers and the beer cans, but there were far too many to pick out, and we looked at the stonework of the foundation, which was weather-beaten and littered with graffiti. I thought it was a bust.

My boyfriend, Chuck, noticed a gnarly old tree about a hundred feet away from the foundation and insisted we go check it out. There weren't any leaves on it and it seemed like it had been dead for years, but there it stood. It was much colder by the tree than it had been at the foundation. Again, we took all kinds of pictures, but as we continued to stay, a mist began forming around us and the tree.
As the mist grew thicker, the tree seemed to take on its own gray glow. It got so cold that we started seeing our breath. That's when the woman appeared. She didn't make any sound, but she walked into the mist retching and convulsing as if she were sick. We stepped away from her, but she looked up at me and all she had for eyes were these deep, dark pits.

We ran out of there as fast as we could.

EXHIBIT 5:
Doctor Patrick's Notes

It must be noted that the full inscription from the stone in Istanbul has two additional lines:

Each man wants to make himself conspicuous and write a book.
The end of the world is manifestly drawing nigh.

Admittedly, I did not include these in my previously published piece, since the bit about book writing seemed extraneous, while the end of the world comment is borderline ridiculous. It merely propounds a psychology of elders that the youth, of whom they do not relate, must be bringing about the end of the world with their changes.

What is interesting to note about these two lines on this particular tablet presented to me is that they're nearly scratched off. It is likely that these scratchings occurred more recently than the original inscription and are not a correction on the part of the author, but I am no forensic expert on the matter.
I am still contemplating the possible purpose for vandalizing these two lines of the inscription and the mindset of one who would do so.

EXHIBIT 6:
The Conover Fire

Conover, Iowa, no longer exists and is classified as a ghost town. Originally intended to be a railway hub, at one point boasting about 200 buildings, including 32 saloons, in 1865, Conover's sparse remnants are now scattered along the outskirts of Calmar.

There was only ever one mayor of Conover, Captain V.C. Jacobs, elected in 1867. The election was controversial, however, as expenses for it exceeded the funds in the town's treasury and the new clerk, J.J. Haug, proceeded to do nothing to repay the debt. Compounding the dire money situation was the continued growth of the railroad to the north and west and the development of Calmar at the eastern terminus and junction.

The town began to dwindle, but the final devastation of Conover came with a great fire that destroyed numerous buildings, including the one serving as the small city hall and courthouse. Scores of important records and documents were destroyed, making the town's history and its financial perils difficult to research. It is noted that town councilmen included Colonel G.O. Pagent, Charles Syndan, and Captain George Q. Gardener, but there is no way to know if they played any significant role in the town's development and demise. The devastation of the fire caused most of the inhabitants to pack up their belongings and buildings and move to Calmar.

There are no records about what caused the fire, just a few notes that it occurred.

EXHIBIT 7:
The Original Inscription?

Dr. Patrick's Notes:

While further delving into the provenance of the tablet, I happened across a dusty text that spoke of a similar inscription, but much more lengthy in scope. This inscription predates the Chaldean one from 3800 B.C. and more likely reigns from Egypt, much closer to 5000 B.C. As is usually the case, older texts are influences for more recent ones; the youth, while separating themselves from their elders, still retain some of the previous generation's history and wisdom while devising their own.

Whoever has ears let them hear,
These are the words of the first and last.

Your afflictions and poverty are known,
All are cast upon a bed of suffering.
Evil times have befallen us,
The world has waxed very old and wicked.
Corruption riddles our kings,
Children usurp their parents.
Every man thinks himself a scribe,
The end of the world is manifestly drawing nigh.
The dead shall walk and shall speak,
Bodies shall be brought forth to the Aged One.
Mothers shall beat their breasts and weep,
All come to the Great House for purification.
Worms feed upon the bodies of men and drink their blood,
Hearts pass through fire and darkness.
Drops of blood shall bring forth the soul,
Storms in the sky burn red.

EXHIBIT 8:
Ghostorian's Journal

This is an excerpt from my personal case journal...

Day 21:

The challenges in this case are many. There is nobody to interview, since the events that transpired around the stone tablet's discovery happened almost 150 years ago. Most of the records from that time were destroyed in a fire. The journal entry that I believe to be the writing of Elijah Dobson was given to me by Dr. Patrick. I find myself cobbling together what few facts remain with the dissection of the local folklore.

One of my jobs as a Ghostorian has been to research and discover the original truth of a tale that has spun into a myth. These stories originated from somewhere, either to explain something that couldn't be explained at the time, or it was a story that morphed out of control in the retelling. With virtually no records available, I am finding it essential to decipher these tales.

A convulsing apparition could correlate to the journal tale of the sickly Elle Dobson, but as far as I can tell that wasn't a part of the local folklore. That was a new report from the woman who answered the inquiry. The local folklore has centered around the foundation and the mist. Yet, that group of people left the foundation to observe an old tree around which the mist formed.

Elijah Dobson spoke of a cottonwood tree in his journal, but cottonwoods only survive about seventy years. At the very most, if the trees are related at all, the current tree could be a seed from the one near the burial site of Elle Dobson and where the tablet was unearthed.

Day 24:

I've been running the few names I have of locals to Conover through the meat grinder of searches to see if I get any hits, but most have proved unfruitful. I found a quick reference to J.J. Haug, a Swiss immigrant, who settled in Marysville, which was later named Calmar after learning there was another town in Iowa named Marysville.

While I didn't find a direct reference to Captain V.C. Jacobs, the mayor of Conover, I did find an 1880 reference to a V. Jacobs at nearby Fort Atkinson as someone holding interest in the old fort's structures, although he was not part of the 1880 census there.

Day 26:

I'm not even sure what to make of this. When I awoke today, I discovered all of the original material that I had received from Dr. Patrick in a heap of ashes on my desk. Nothing else was touched or burned, but everything from him was destroyed. Fortunately, I had made copies and my records are intact, but the fact that just one pile of material went up in smoke—and the smoke alarm did not go off—is absolutely bizarre. There is nothing to salvage, but I am storing the ash in a plastic container for who knows what future purpose.

Day 31:

My searching has not been in vain after all. I was placed in contact today with a woman who claims to be a decedent of Charles Syndan, who briefly served on the council of Conover. She was reluctant to talk much at all about her great-grandfather, but she thought it important that I listen to the brief tales she had been told of his time in Conover.

The record of her tale from our phone conversation:

Grandpa Charles was a private man, but he had a few tales he would spin. Some, I'm sure, were great yarns, and every once in a while he would talk about this little town that no longer exists known as Conover. He only spent a short spell there

[story continued on following page]

serving as a councilman, but that time was enough for him. The town was broke and the promises from the railroad had been broken. Conover was going to go belly up, which was of great dismay to the mayor, who was newly elected and was quite enjoying his little reign of power, small as it was. He was frantic in trying to figure out how to bring money back into the town to keep the business there. Most of it was in saloons from the connections to the railroad that was leaving, so Grandpa Charles wasn't confident anything could seriously be done.

Well, suddenly, the mayor called a meeting of the council to talk to them about a story he'd heard from the Reverend about some ancient artifact that one of the locals had dug up. He thought if there was history buried out in the cow pastures of Conover, then the town could attract the business of a different sort in the scholars and intellectuals of the day. He was laughed right out of the meeting house.

Now, Grandpa Charles, while he didn't believe any sort of migration of scholars to Conover was even probable, let alone could save the town. He was interested in this story he'd heard about an ancient relic. What exactly was it and where did it come from? He found the mayor and the Reverend in a heated argument in a back room of one of the saloons, carrying on about who should have ownership of this artifact. The Reverend insisted such things belonged in the hands of the church, while the mayor argued that it was an object of history and science, not to be trapped by the Church, and they should use it and anything else they unearthed to found a university.

"I'd rather see this town burn in hell!" Grandpa Charles overheard the Reverend yell.

Now, the very next day, the town did burn down, or, at least, most of it. Grandpa Charles was sure the Reverend had held true to his word, but to Grandpa's dismay, when the mayor addressed the town after the fire, he claimed children had accidentally started a fire behind one of the saloons.

Nobody questioned the matter and Conover was soon abandoned, but Grandpa Charles always believed the Reverend was the one that set the blaze. As for the ancient artifact that was supposed to have been discovered on the land, well, my great-grandfather never did learn exactly what that was or where it ended up. Most people moved to Calmar and lived out the rest of their days in peace, while others moved on their own separate ways completely.

EXHIBIT 9:
The Formicarius

Dr. Patrick's Notes:

From the identical source as I had received the stone tablet, I have received into my possession another peculiar object: a translated copy of *The Formicarius* of Johannes Nider. The text is quite unfamiliar to me and dates to the 1420s. I was instructed to note the following passages:

There are, or there very recently were (as both the same inquisitor and Lord Peter have told me, and as is well known among the public) in the territory of Bern, a great many witches of both sexes who greatly hated human nature and assumed the likenesses of various kinds of beasts, especially those kinds that devour children.

In the town of Boltingen, in the diocese of Lausanne, there lived a man named Stadelin, a great witch, who was arrested by the same Lord Peter, the judge of the district. Stadelin had

[story continued on following page]

entered a house where a man and wife lived and by his witch-craft killed seven successive infants in her womb.

After this fashion was I seduced, and my wife also, whom I believe of so great pertinacity that she will endure the flames rather than confess the least whit of truth, but alas, we are both guilty. What the young man was seen to die in great contrition. His wife, however, though convicted by the testimony of witnesses, would not confess the truth even under the torture or in death; but, when the fire was prepared for her by the executioner, she uttered in most evil words a curse upon him, and was so burned.

Finally, this year I learned from the aforesaid inquisitor that in the duchy of Lausanne, certain witches cooked their own newly born babies, and ate them. Moreover, the means of learning such art was, so he said, that the witches came together in a certain convocation, and through their efforts, they saw a demon visibly in an assumed human form, to whom the disciple had to pledge that he would deny Christianity, would never adore the Eucharist, and would secretly trample on the cross whenever he could.

These two knew how to carry over a third part of the dung, hay, or grain, or whatever sort of things, when it pleased them, from their neighbor's field to their own field, with no one seeing them, how to raise enormous hailstorms and destructive winds with lightning, how to hurl children walking near water, in the sight of their parents, into that with no one seeing them, how to bring sterility in people and animals, and how to harm those near them both bodily and in goods.

EXHIBIT 10:
Ghostorian's Notes on the Formicarius

Pre-Note:

Before I get into my notes on *The Formicarius*, I think it would be wise to note that just before Dr. Patrick presented me with the text, I spotted a little girl spying on me through the window of my office. She was in an old weather-beaten dress and she looked rather sad. I ran outside to talk to her, but she was gone by the time I got to where she had been standing by the window. Now, thinking back on the girl, the dress she was wearing was extremely outdated.

The Formicarius is a precursor to the *Malleus Maleficarum* [The Witch's Hammer] and is said to have heavily influenced it. Aside from two minor points, why it has suddenly been thrust into the mix of this mystery is beyond me.

The tales of witchcraft in Nider's *Formicarius* are largely focused in areas of Switzerland. A number of the inhabitants of the area around Conover were Swiss immigrants. Perhaps they brought this old tome with them.
There's also the little one-liner ghost sighting from the area:

There's the foundation of an old witch's house near Calmar that is haunted by a freezing white mist on some nights, even though it's warm outside.

At first, I figured the description of a witch's house was conjecture on the part of the teller, or mythology added into the mix over the years of the reported mist. When people tell tales of seeing things, they like to add in their own explanations for the occurrence, which after many re-tellings over time, suddenly become a pseudo-fact of the event. This could still be the case, but perhaps a deeper reason why this is the case is because the culture of the people who lived there included

[story continued on following page]

stories of witches. Granted, we're talking a time period about 450 years after *The Formicarius* was written, but some cultural traits stick around for a long time. After all, my own Swiss ancestors fled to America in the late 1600s due to religious persecution, already more than 150 years from its authorship. I also find it interesting, in my brief research of Johannes Nider, that some of the more extensive materials covering the subject were books coming out of Iowa State University.

EXHIBIT 11:
Ghostorian's Journal

Day 36:

Doctor Patrick has disappeared. I had been unable to contact him the past couple days, which led me to seek him out at the hotel he'd been staying at. There was no answer at the door, so I asked the clerk at the service desk if the doctor had left. The clerk gave me a perplexed look and told me that he had never heard of Dr. Patrick and nobody had rented that room in weeks, since it had been sealed off for renovation.

I went home puzzled and unsure what to do. I had assembled this web of history and tales that didn't make a whole lot of sense, and the one that had requested my help with it had vanished as if he'd never existed. I was dumbfounded even more when I returned home and found *The Formicarius* text I'd received from Dr. Patrick in a heap of ashes on my desk. Again, nothing else had been damaged.

EXHIBIT 12:
The Lost Journal

Ghostorian's Note:

A small leather-bound journal showed up in my mail with no return address. It had only one entry:

Perhaps I should have just stolen the tablet from Dobson. Now who knows where it is. It's gone, and maybe it's no longer a part of this physical earthly plane. It would have been a prize in the hands of anyone with a bit of sense, instead of that bumbling fool and his family. Instead, it got a hold of that little girl. Children started a fire behind a saloon, indeed. It was one child, the youngest one, in fact, but it may not really have been her. I think I saw the devil in her eyes. The flames behind her rose in a motley sea of colors, and it spread from building to building like wildfire. I thought the world was ending as the skies stormed red. She calmly stalked the road through the middle of town,

holding that great weight of a tablet. I have no idea how she managed it.

Of few that saw her other than I, some screamed "witch," while others screamed "demon," and each that did, perished. I believe my silence saved me from her wrath while all others fled. Throughout the terror, I stood still and silent and watched as she stoically walked straight out of Conover.

It was such a striking difference from the meek little girl that I observed in the window of her home, another time I stood silent and watched. I had stopped by the farm seeking a small contribution, and Elle was there only with the little one. Elijah was out working his field and the other children must have been off at school, but Rogers was there. I don't know what he shoved down the throat of that woman, but he made sure to tell her, "I know your husband lied about my horse, now he's not going to have his own horse no more!"

[story continued on following page]

I didn't realize until Elle died that he was insulting her at the same time by calling her a horse. I thought he was just taking a hand to her and Elijah would see and deal with it. I expected one of Elijah's horses to show up dead, but no. I suppose it was one of many things I didn't understand throughout this entire tragedy. I didn't understand and I didn't act. I just stood silent and still and I didn't tell Dobson what Rogers had done.

And for it, my town that had been my dream is now gone.

-V.C. Jacobs

EXHIBIT 13:
Final Thoughts

Day 42:

This case is as open as it is closed. There are a myriad of loose ends that I don't expect will be tied up anytime soon, and I'm not sure I want to devote the time it would take into doing that right now.

I still have heard nothing of the mysterious Dr. Patrick, where he went and, really, where he had even come from. Just as quickly as he had come into my life, he vanished. However, who is not vanishing is the little girl.

I will see her on occasion peering through the window at me as I work in my office. I waved to her once and she ran. I've noticed after multiple times seeing her now, that her vintage mid-nineteenth century dress is dotted with droplets of dried blood and singed around the edges, as if it had suffered a little fire damage. I've since been calling her Mary.

I don't know what may have happened to her after the Conover fire and if there is any rest for her soul. Perhaps she is looking for the tablet and thinks that Dr. Patrick gave it to me, but he never did and I have no idea where it may be. Perhaps there is a connection between the tablet and her mother that she seeks, since her mother's body replaced the resting place of the tablet.

Like I said, there are too many loose ends.

There is still a longing, however, to uncover the origins of the tablet and its inscription and why it, apparently, holds such power. I expect whatever secrets it holds are as potent now as they were then—it always seems to be evil times, after all.

-Mike Ricksecker
Ghostorian

The Gateway
to Hell

Stull, KS

A clank emanated from before them, the circular stone seemingly pulled back into the wall, and the wall itself fell back to reveal a black staircase descending deep underground

Is this one of the seven gateways to hell?

"Ellis, baby, look at this."

Jasmine Smith dropped a thick, leather-bound tome in front of her husband, Ellis, as he drank his morning coffee in the comfort of their new home.

He cocked an eyebrow at the massive, ancient volume and took another sip of coffee. "Up bright and early rummaging through the attic?"

"That attic is just loaded with old treasures. You really ought to have a look up there."

"Nah. To me one man's junk is another man's junk."

Jasmine shook her head. "It was just an old spinster woman that lived here. It wasn't one man's nothing."

"An old spinster woman?"

"That's right."

"So in the middle of Kansas, an old spinster woman lived in a hundred-year-old farm house? Go figure that. Her bones are probably rolling over in her grave knowing that a brother is now living in her house."

Jasmine waved a dismissive hand at her husband. "Oh, you stop being like that. There's good people here."

"Good people?" Ellis pushed away his coffee mug. "We only know your friend, Wendy, and you really hadn't seen her since LSU. Come on, baby. We're probably the only African-American couple within fifty miles of this place."

"That friend, Wendy, helped both of us find jobs up here, remember?"

"Yeah, well, why couldn't she help find us ones closer to Lafayette?"

Jasmine pushed the large, dusty book toward her husband. "You know how the economy has been. Now stop your whining and have a look at this."

Ellis cocked his eyebrow at the book again, but didn't touch it. "What is it?"

"It's fascinating is what it is!" Jasmine creaked open the first couple yellowed pages. "Look at how old this must be with all the intricate script."

"This is your history major coming out in you, isn't it? Is that even English?"

Jasmine rolled her yes. "Yes, it's English. It's just old. And I think it's some sort of witchcraft."

"Oh, no you don't. Don't be bringing your grandmother's voodoo up in here."

"You stop that. Just because I have Creole blood in me does not mean that my grandmama was into voodoo. What's the matter with you, Ellis? This is a historic find! It's not like witchcraft is real."

"What makes you think it's witchcraft?"

Jasmine shrugged. "Its not my historic expertise at all, but the way these read, they look like incantations."

Ellis pushed away the book much the same as he had his coffee mug. "Then I suggest you just out it away. Donate it to a museum. We don't need to be getting cursed."

"Cursed! Oh, you're just being superstitious."

Ellis rose and placed a hand on his wife's shoulder. "No. We're just starting a new life here. I'm just being safe."

Wendy Carson had never seen anything like it, but she was absolutely enthralled. Covered in decades of dust, the relic must have been about four inches thick and nearly the same width and height as a standard sheet of paper. The book was huge, heavy, and the leatherwork on the cover bore its own intricate design.

"What are those circles and loops on the cover?" Wendy asked her long-time friend from college, Jasmine.

"I have no idea. I thought you might know something about it, since everyone seems to know everyone around here. Did Ms. Pendegrast never say anything about the book, or witchcraft, or anything like that?"

Wendy sighed. "She was probably the most reclusive woman in the whole town. In a place like this, everyone does know each other, like you said, but Ms. Pendegrast was probably the one person nobody really knew."

Jasmine sighed. "Lovely."

The two friends stared at the volume resting on the coffee table before them. Jasmine's curiosity was heightened and she felt as if the book was almost calling out to her. She loved old objects and rummaging through antique stores. It's why she was now a history teacher. She loved the stories behind the history and the long journey things like this book had to take to get where they are now. To Jasmine, and old dresser had a set of eyes that had once gazed upon a long-forgotten era and held secrets to a past to which no one continued to pay attention.

Jasmine sat upright and grabbed Wendy's hand. "Strength in sisters!"

"Oh, no you don't!" Wendy tried to retract her hand, but Jasmine's grip was too tight.

"Oh, yes, I am!"

"I'm not 21 anymore, Jazz, and neither are you."

"Oh, come on. It wasn't even ten years ago. We're doing this."

Wendy shook her head in vain. "Look, no, Frank—"

"—doesn't need to know. Just tell him you're showing me around the town. It's kind of the truth anyway, but while you're showing me around, we're going to get to the bottom of this."

"Crap."

The tiny library branch had seen better days. Dusty and musty, it looked like the small stacks hadn't seen a new book since the Reagan administration. For that matter, it appeared the librarian's tenure may have predated Nixon. She shuffled forward to a small counter that served both circulation and reference, and she peered at the two women over half moon reading glasses.

"How may I help you young ladies?"

Jasmine heaved the tome she had recovered from the attic to the top of the counter and asked, "Do you know anything about this book or one like it?"

The elderly woman stepped back and stammered, "I—no. No. Where did you find this? Wendy James Carson, you ought to be ashamed of yourself!"

Wendy blushed and slunk behind Jasmine. "I'm sorry, Mrs. Knox. Ashamed of what?"

The librarian straightened her glasses. "For stealing that—that thing!"

Jasmine leaned across the counter. "We didn't steal anything. I found this in my attic, and I want to know more about it."

"Your attic?" Mrs. Know shook her head. "Ms. Pendegrast's attic? But that can't be."

"Why not?"

"Because it's been locked away safely in the vault here for more than twenty years!" The librarian pointed a steely finger at the two women. "You're looking to meddle in things that are not of your concern. Perhaps you're just curious and really have no idea of the things that happen down in Stull, but I'm warning you to get out now. Leave the book here and I'll have it put back where it belongs. Leave the book here and you'll be safe. Just go teach the kiddies about George Washington and leave the real history to those of us that know better."

Jasmine and Wendy exchanged worried glances, and Jasmine grabbed the book off the counter. "I think we'll be going now."

They headed straight for the door, but Mrs. Knox called after them, "I'm going to have to report this as a theft, little missy. And, Wendy, what would your mother say?"

Wendy straightened. "My mother is dead, Mrs. Knox. She won't be saying anything."

Once outside, they jumped in Wendy's car and careened out of the small library parking lot. Jasmine held tightly to the tome and looked at her friend, whose eyes were fixated on the road ahead.

"That was some backbone, Wendy. I never said this about you because I never wanted to hurt your feelings, but you were always the more timid of our group back in the day. I'm impressed. Life after college must have done you some good."

Wendy shook her head. "No. You're right. I'm shy and timid and usually let people walk all over me. But she didn't need to bring my mother into this. Mrs. Knox was there at the funeral, as was most of the town, and dragging my mother into this was just meant to hurt me and guilt trip me. There's a lot of things with me you can use to do that, but my deceased mother is not one of them."

Within moments they had exited the two-stoplight town.

"I guess this is it."

Wendy inched her car up the narrow, single-lane gravel path into the cemetery and stopped just inside the gate. Headstones dotted the small hill in neat little rows and Wendy sighed.

Jasmine scrolled through an article on her cell phone. "This has got to be the connection—the Stull Cemetery and one of the seven gateways to hell."

"Stull, Kansas? Really?"

"Really. Well, that's according to all these legends. Historically, there's not a lot of truth behind the legends that I'm digging up, but if Mrs. Knox haphazardly said Stull, well, this is all I'm finding."

"Which is exactly what?"

"According to legend, there is a stairway to hell on the property near where the old church had once stood. The entrance is supposed to be difficult to find, sealed by a slab somewhere near the building, but once found you descend the stairwell and time is... altered, I suppose. Some say that if you venture down the steps for just a few moments, weeks will really pass. There are a number of comments about the church being used for devil and occult worship and the devil supposedly has made appearances at the cemetery. Also, an old pine tree that grew just inside the cemetery is said to have hung witches, but there are no facts to back that up, of course.

In reality, it is an old Methodist church that simply moved down the road in 1922. Likely, the crumbling ruins caused people to create all kinds of spooky stories. I see that all the time. The building was bulldozed just a couple years ago. The only truths of the pine tree I can find are that it did split a headstone belonging to a married couple that died in 1879, and it was cut down just before Halloween in 1998 after having lived for a hundred years.

There are a couple other legends of the area along a road that no longer exists, and it was supposed to have been called Devil's Road. This says that near there, in the early 1900s, a young boy was accidentally burned to death by his father and a man was once found hanging from a tree. If that was truly named Devil's Road, then there could be some transference in the tales from there to the abandoned church and the old tree. That happens, too."

Wendy turned off the car and shook her head. "That's a lot to take in. So, if you believe these are all just tales then what exactly are we doing here?"

Jasmine pointed at the book resting on the back seat. "We have that and the librarian said Stull."

They exited the car and started walking down the gravel path in search of the spot at which the old church had once stood.

Wendy still had questions. "So let's say we find this staircase. Then what?"

Jasmine laughed. "I don't know. It's all part of the adventure, girl! You see, this is what I love about history. You have these fantastic old tales, stories of people's lives and events, some true and some not, and here we are seeking the truth. Some of the most interesting exploration we have today is into our own pasts and figuring out where it is we really came from, how all of these things came to be. And sometimes the truth is more shocking than the tales."

"Um, I guess that would be it." Wendy pointed to a pile of rubble at the top of the hill off the gravel road.

The two friends circled the remains multiple times, examining the heap of old stone but finding nothing of real interest. The wind kicked up and whipped about their ears, repeatedly blowing Wendy's long, sandy-brown hair into her face.

She spit a strand of hair out of her mouth. "There's nothing here, Jasmine. It's just a demolished building and a bunch of headstones."

Jasmine stood on the gravel path before the rubble with her hands on her hips. "Then why did she say, 'Stull?' I'm going to get the book. Maybe there's something in there to help us."

"Jazz..."

Moments later, Jasmine returned with the dusty book in hand and started leafing through the pages. Already she could tell something was different.

"Wendy, put your hand on this and feel it."

Wendy placed her hand on the open pages and her eyes shot up at her friend. "It's like its vibrating."

"Yeah, that's crazy. Isn't it? I have an idea."

With the ancient tome in hand the two women circled the remnants of the old building and detected noticeable changes in the vibration as they neared certain areas. There was one particular corner, however, in which the small vibrations of the book picked up speed.

Jasmine glanced about. "It must be around here somewhere."

Wendy pulled wind-blown hair out of her face. "Around where? I really don't see anything but broken stone."

"The stairway is supposed to go into the ground covered by a slab just outside the church building. Here you see that some of the stone has spilled outside the walls. I bet it's under here."

"A slab? So even if we find this thing we're not going to be able to get into it."

"Nonsense. You have a tire iron in your car, right?"

Wendy sighed and, together, they began moving bits of the rubble. It was laborious work, but they soon had a four foot square section cleared out and were staring at a narrow rectangular stone set into the ground. Its surface was rough cut, but generally flat.

Jasmine stretched. "I bet that's it. Doesn't look big. From what I read, it used to be very difficult to find; I guess there must have been foliage here at some point, but the stone from the building would have crushed it and killed it off."

"It's not like that was easy. I guess I'll get the tire iron and a flashlight from the roadside kit. I can't believe we're doing this."

A few minutes later, they were staring at a narrow stone staircase that descended into the earth before them. The depths were dark, the bottom of the stairwell unviewable.

Jasmine smiled at her friend. "Let's go to hell."

The two friends stared at the four walls, downtrodden and discouraged. They had driven far and worked hard, but they had not been rewarded for their efforts. Musty and dusty, much like the book that rested in Jasmine's hand, they found themselves in an empty square room, likely sealed off from the public for decades.

"So, what exactly is this, Jazz?"

Jasmine sighed. "It's just a storeroom. Perishable items would have been kept down here, maybe wine. This really isn't uncommon for old churches. I should have known better than to listen to silly legends and go digging around here."

Wendy put an arm around her friend. "Oh, don't say that. Remember what you told me earlier about finding the real truth behind the legends? You've done just that. There really is a staircase here, but it's just that it leads to a storeroom. Let's go home."

"Maybe you're right."

"Sure, of course. This was actually a pretty cool day. The only thing I still wonder about is why the book vibrates the way it does."

Jasmine looked down at the strange leather designs of the closed book and shook her head. "I have no idea."

"Hey! Look at that."

"What?"

Wendy was pointing at the far wall. "Why is that stone straight ahead of us circular? All the others are rectangular?"

"I...I don't know. It's odd, for sure. But this place is old, so maybe during the construction they just used what they could find."

Jasmine approached the circular stone set into the wall, and as she did so the leather circular designs on the book cover began to glow a soft orange.

"Are you kidding me? Wendy, look at this!"

Wendy stepped up beside her friend and gasped. The glow grew brighter and the design became clearer while the stone in the wall also began to glow orange. Jasmine placed her hand to the book cover and tugged one of the loops. A clank emanated from before them, the circular stone seemingly pulled back into the wall, and the wall itself fell back to reveal a black staircase descending deep underground. Torches lined the walls and a sulfuric odor rose up from below which glowed a deep red-orange.

Jasmine inched backward. "Okay, I think we've taken this far enough."

Wendy's mouth fell open. "Really? Look at where you've led us, and you're just going to walk away now?"

"Yes, that's enough."

"I don't believe you, talking about adventure the way you were. You don't get to back out now."

"This is different. Wendy, no!"

Jasmine's cries fell upon deaf ears as her friend bolted for the staircase and disappeared into the fiery glow. Jasmine tossed the book to the side and followed after, plunging down the staircase that bore deep into the earth. It quickly became sweltering hot, steam rose around her on all sides as she descended further, and the stench became more rank. Step after blackened step she plodded, screaming Wendy's name into the nothing of the endless passage. Time did seem to slip away, for Jasmine did not know how long it had been when she finally reached a landing. The stair continued on the other side, but Wendy was there at the landing with what looked like an older version of herself.

"Wendy! What on earth are you doing, girl?"

With a large grin, Wendy approached Jasmine with the older woman, an arm draped over her shoulder. "Jasmine, I'd like you to meet my mother."

"Your mother?"

"Yes. I can't thank you enough for all you've done to bring me here to get her."

Jasmine's eyes darted between Wendy and her mother. They bore a strikingly similar resemblance aside from the age factor, but what disconcerted Jasmine were her mother's eyes. While Wendy's were a plain brown, her mother's were a brilliant hazel with an extraordinarily glossy sheen.

"What do you mean to get her? You mean you knew about this place all along?"

Wendy laughed. "Of course! Everyone around here knows the legend, and if you volunteer long enough at the library as a kid you might just learn about the old book hidden away in the vault."

"You stole the book? And you put it in the attic of my new house? Wendy Carson, what have you done?"

"I did what I had to in order to bring my mother back."

A fire began to rage within Jasmine. "Why me?"

"I knew you couldn't resist. When we were at LSU, there was a time when you couldn't stop talking about the Myrtles Plantation. I knew you'd be a sucker for something like this. The fact that you're part Creole was a bonus. Makes for a better sacrifice."

Jasmine turned to run back up the stairs, but Wendy's mother grabbed her shoulder from behind and stopped her dead in her tracks. The strength in just a single hand grip was like a vise.

"Mother isn't going to let you just get away like that."

Jasmine struggled to get away and make a break for the stairs, but was unable to wrest free. "Wendy, I don't think that's your mother. You don't know what you're messing with here."

"I know exactly what I'm doing. Just because I'm from a small Kansas town doesn't mean I don't know what I'm doing. Didn't you hear Mrs. Knox? Leave the real history to those of us that know better."

Jasmine was tossed to the side like a rag doll and mother and daughter ascended the staircase. With blood trickling from her forehead, Jasmine dusted herself off and raced after. She had no idea what she could possibly do, but she wouldn't let the devil loose upon the world without putting up a fight.

The stairs were a hard grind upward and onward, and her legs screamed in searing agony, but Jasmine was gaining on them. She never thought those morning jogs would be good for anything more than just keeping the pounds off, but here she was chasing Wendy and her demon mother—or whatever she was—up the endless flight of stairs out of hell. Stair after stair the climb seemed like it would never end, but she finally reached the top and was back in the small storage room where Wendy and the mother figure were just exiting the other side.

"Wendy!"

Wendy's mother turned to Jasmine with a twisted, sickening grin and waved her hand. Jasmine was lifted off the ground with a force that slammed her into an adjacent stone wall. Shards of light blazed in Jasmine's eyes as she fell and her head cracked onto the floor.

Wendy turned to the battered body of her friend lying in a heap. "You're making this more difficult than it has to be, Jazz. Your fate is sealed and you will take my mother's place, but if you keep this up I will make sure your husband burns with you, too!"

Jasmine had heard enough. She wiped the blood dripping from her head out of her eyes and started to rise, but then realized wedged underneath her body was the old book that had brought them here to begin with. She pulled it out from under her and began muttering words that she had heard her grandmother utter long ago when she was a little girl. It was like a dream, out in the bayou somewhere, she and her grandmother and a circle of others. Words that she faintly recalled fell out of her mouth and she slammed her blood-soaked hand upon the book.

A dazzling white light suddenly shone from above the small staircase that led back outside and the entire room was bathed in its brilliance. Wendy and her mother looked up in terror and covered their eyes as the piercing luminance bore down upon them. An elderly African-American woman emerged from the radiant light rays, grabbed Wendy's mother by the collar, and threw her down the stairway to hell. Screams blared from the stairwell as the wall rose back into place and sealed the gateway once again.

The African-American woman placed a gentle hand upon Jasmine's cheek and a flash of frolicking in the springtime, warm cornbread, and fresh crawdads came to mind.

"Grandmama?"

"Hush, child."

Jasmine smiled and the pain from her wounds faded. Slowly, the light subsided and she was alone in the small storeroom with Wendy. She stepped toward the woman that once called her friend and held out her hand, palm up.

"The keys to your car, please."

"Jasmine, I'm...I'm sorry. I just wanted my mother—"

"Your keys."

Wendy handed Jasmine the keys to her car and Jasmine punched Wendy dead in the face.

"I can't say that I appreciate you storming out of here yesterday, but I thank you for returning the book."

Jasmine nodded and left the old tome on the counter in the library. "I apologize for the misunderstanding, Mrs. Knox. You're right. I still have a lot to learn."

"Yes, you do."

Mrs. Knox was grateful for the book having been returned, but scolded Jasmine all the same. This was not the first time someone had tried to steal the book, and it wouldn't be the last.

Jasmine returned home, where she and Ellis began making plans for an immediate move back to Lafayette. They would figure out the economics when they got back to familiar territory.

That night, however, in the dark recesses of the iron vault at the library, the circular designs on the cover of the dusty, old book began to glow orange once again.

The Legend Beneath
the Coal Bin

Cuyahoga County, OH

...a blood-curdling scream ripped
through the entire house.
"Aiiieee!"

"Do you really expect me to believe that this is going to work?"

"That's what the book said." I grinned at my cousin, Mandy, as the four of us held the feather-covered rods out in front of us. "If the rods cross on their own, then there's an Indian buried right where we're standing."

We inched further into the coal bin, small clouds of dust billowing before us as we shuffled across the floor, when suddenly the two rods crossed.

"Oh my God!"

It was only supposed to be a joke to scare my sister and our younger cousin, but I never suspected that the legend I created would change our lives forever.

In the twelfth summer of my youth, stranded at my grandparents' house with nothing more to do than to play with the old wig in the attic, I devised a plan that I knew would surely scare the girls. Rifling through the dusty encyclopedias that lined the stairs, I settled upon the dark story of the Shawnee Indian, Tenskwatawa. In his day, he was known as "The Prophet," a holy man who preached of the "Great Spirit" and "Master of Life" and condemned people of witchcraft, including an old woman that he slowly burned at the stake for four days. Dependence on goods, such as guns, iron cookware, glass beads, and alcohol from white settlers were seen as horrific sins in his eyes. He teamed with his brother, Tecumseh, in forming a Native American confederation against the whites pushing west. Citing that the Master of Life would guarantee victory, Tenswatawa was routed at Tippecanoe by future President William Henry Harrison, but that's where my story changed. In my story, Tenskwatawa was brutally killed in the same small town that my grandparents lived. In my story, President William Henry Harrison died in office by the curse of Tenskwatawa.

With the help of Mark, the ten-year-old that lived next door, we crafted cryptic messages on remnants of old scrap paper and strategically placed them where the girls would offhandedly discover them. We laughed in secret when my sister, Tammy, ran to us, panting, with the first scrawled note in her hand.

As the mystery deepened for Tammy and Mandy, we needed more information about the Indian Prophet than the encyclopedia could provide. Mark helped us with a raggedy leather-bound journal that he stumbled across at the library. The pages were ancient and crackled when we turned them, but they let us see through another's eyes the fire that Tenskwatawa brought with him. Near the back of the journal was the strange description of finding the buried body of a fallen tribesman. By taking two rods an arm's length long, each with six feathers attached to it, and holding them out from the body, the grave seeker patrols the area where he suspects the body to be. If the rods cross, the journal states a Shawnee Indian is buried there. Naturally, we told Tammy and Mandy that the body of Tenskwatawa was buried beneath our grandparents' basement and we were going to find him. I just hadn't suspected that I might actually be right.

I stopped dead in my tracks and stared open-mouthed at the rods, but continued to play along. "Did the note say anything about being buried in the coal bin?"

Mandy trembled. "No, it just said underneath the basement."

Tammy frowned. "But I thought Indian burial grounds were supposed to have a lot of bodies. This is just one."

Mark quickly countered, "Maybe that means he was important and was buried in a special place."

Mandy began biting her nails. "Maybe it's Tenskwatawa."

Tammy scowled. "Maybe it's just some dumb guy that got lost in the woods."

"I know how we can find out," blurted Mark. Everyone stared at him, afraid of what he may actually suggest.

"We're not going to dig him up," Mandy stammered.

"No, the journal." Mark nodded his head in the direction of the floor above us where the book had been laid. "At the end of it is a ritual for raising the spirit of an Indian. It's supposed to send them on their way to the Great Spirit."

No one said anything. We all continued to simply stare at Mark, unable to fathom what would be involved with raising a restless Native American spirit hundreds of years old.

He elaborated, "If I remember right, we'll need the feathers from these rods, a handful of earth, and a drop of blood. I guess one of us could prick their finger with something. Then there are some words we're supposed to say. Won't this be so cool?"

Still, we just stared at Mark as if he were some sort of bizarre creature from another world. Suddenly, something fell against the far wall and we all jumped out of our shoes. Mandy crept back toward the door and clung to the frame, ready to bolt to the safety of upstairs. Mark shot me a bewildered look, as if he thought I had done something to create the noise. I shrugged and inched toward the wall to see what had fallen.

The replacement of the old coal furnace decades before I was born had left the coal bin destined to be a junk storage room. It was filled with broken sets of golf clubs, crumbling furniture covered with dust, and jars of something Grandma had cooked up before the war. When I prodded through the golf clubs, something furry darted across the floor into an old bowling shoe and we all screamed.

"It's just a mouse," Tammy spat. "I'm outta here."

She stormed away with Mandy right on her heels. Mark and I gave the coal bin one final look and we reluctantly trailed behind.

"Let's do it tonight," Mark insisted later that evening after dinner. "I'm sleeping over anyway. It's the perfect time."

"No way." I closed the door to the bedroom so we could discuss in secret. "We were only doing all of this for a few laughs."

"But what if it *is* Tenskwatawa?"

"Then we'd better leave him there. He wasn't exactly a nice guy."

"But this is a chance to meet a real live Indian, not something like we see on TV. When I was at the library, there was all kinds of cool stuff about Native Americans and how they lived."

I punched Mark in the shoulder with a friendly jab. "Except he's not a real live Indian, numbskull. He's dead, in the ground! We shouldn't mess with that no matter how much we want to scare Tammy and Mandy."

Mark grunted in frustration. "But then we could see what he was really like! The little painting we saw of him was pretty awesome. He could teach us stuff."

"Tenskwatawa, back in the day, would have been cool. Zombie Tenskwatawa today, not so much."

Mark dropped the subject after that, but something told me he wasn't really done with the matter. In fact, as we went to bed that night, I could have sworn I saw him tuck the old journal under his pillow.

Thump-thump.

I rolled over in bed and groggily squinted at the clock. 3:02 a.m.

Thump-thump.

"Aw, who left the TV on?" I wearily called out into the darkness.

Thump-thump, thump-thump.

"You hear that, Mark? Mark?" I rolled back over and peered at the other bed where Mark was supposed to be sleeping. He wasn't there.

Thump-thump, thump-thump.

My mind started racing, trying to place the sound as the thumping became steadier, like the repetitious beat of a—drum!

Thump-thump, thump-thump, thump-thump.

It was a leather-skinned drum like the ones Native Americans would beat on as they prepared for war. I leaped out of my bed as the thumping grew louder, threw on my robe, and was about to grab the doorknob when a blood-curdling scream ripped through the entire house.

"Aiiieee!"

I ripped open the door and dashed down the stairs, nearly plowing over my father, who had also awoken to the beating drum that had now suddenly stopped. Lights were being thrown on everywhere in the wake of the nerve-racking scream that still echoed through the walls. My father and I tore through the kitchen and down the basement steps, the rest of the household barreling right along behind us.

What we saw down there was unimaginable and has been left as a scar upon my very soul. A blue light dazzled from the coal bin and a Native American wearing a red headdress danced within its rays with a fresh scalp in his hand. He chanted words we didn't understand as he spun around, then stopped and stared at us, holding out the scalp. He shrilled out an ear-splitting laugh and in a flash he was gone.

No one knows how long we stood motionless on the steps, but it seemed like hours. Finally, my father slowly ventured into the coal bin and returned with six feathers speckled with blood and the old leather-bound journal.

Mark was never seen again and to this very day the police still believe he ran away. The coal bin was boarded up and my grandparents placed an old heavy dresser in front of the door so no one would dare try to enter again. My family never talks of that night and the tragedy that fell upon it. But sometimes on a hot and hazy summer night, when the destitute wind is still, one can distinctly hear the *thump-thump* of a drum echoing from the dark recesses of the old coal bin.

Church of Darkness

(Black Bear Creek, OK)

When you walk in, it feels like all eyes are upon you. You see the shadows peering in through the windows—short, stout shadow figures, just barely taller than the bottom of the windows, boring holes into you.

Illuminated balls of light are often captured at the old Black Bear Church.

Leonard Gammel cracked open his front door under the weight of heavy reluctance. He wanted no part of the man standing on the stoop, just as he had wanted no part of his wife's paranormal team, a hobby that Leonard thought Shelby could do without. However, this man was waiting there on behalf of his wife's friend from Massachusetts, and you didn't say "no" to the type of money she could throw at the situation.

"Mr. Gammel?"

Leonard stepped back. Was this guy for real? A long, leather trench coat draped over shoulders and a black fedora adorned his head. Did he step out of the 1940s or had Leonard stepped through some sort of time warp when he opened the door? All this guy was missing was the cigarette and the dame.

"Yeah, I'm Leonard Gammel."

The stranger extended his hand. "I'm Chase Michael DeBarlo, a private detective from Fallsbury, Massachusetts. I was hired by Genelle Starr to look into your wife's disappearance."

They shook and Leonard invited the character into his modest Dallas-style home. Moments later, in front of the crackling embers of a wood burning fireplace, he was telling the detective the very little he knew about his wife's disappearance.

"I don't know what to tell you, because I really didn't want to hear much of the crazy things she'd been

The ruins of what was once the New Bethany Baptist Church.

talking about. She got up with one of those paranormal teams, like the kind you see on TV, and I really don't believe in that sort of thing. Then she started ranting and raving about all these crazy dreams she'd been having, but I just told her they were only dreams. So, yeah, her behavior was different lately—and then she was just gone."

Chase was writing the few details down on a small notepad he had pulled out from the interior pocket of his trench coat. "Tell me more about this paranormal team."

Leonard shrugged. "Like I said, I don't know what to tell you. They were into ghosts and going into people's homes that had spooked themselves into thinking their house was haunted."

"And you don't believe in that sort of thing?"

"Nah. I only believe in what I can see with my own eyes."

"Do you have a way I can contact this team?"

"Yeah. It's called Society of the Haunted. I got the number for one of the other members in the kitchen. The cops wanted that, too, but they all got alibis and there's no motive they can find at this point if, say, one of them kidnapped her."

"What do you think happened?"

Leonard shook his head. He didn't want to say it, but it had been nagging the back of his mind for days. "I think she ran off with some guy."

"What guy?"

He shook his head again. "I don't know. Some guy. When she wasn't doing all that ghost stuff she was online chatting with all sorts of different people, including a lot of different guys."

DeBarlo rested his pencil on top of his notebook and leaned forward. "Any guy in particular?"

"Nah, I don't know. She said it was all innocent stuff and I had nothing to worry about, but I knew she'd done some flirting around, so you never know."

"You seem rather nonchalant about it."

"I'm nonchalant about nothing. If she did run off with some guy, then I'd rip out his nuts. I just can't think of any other reason, as unreasonable as it may seem to some."

The detective stood up. "Mind if I have a look around? Maybe I can check out this computer she was chatting on, that sort of thing."

Leonard grunted. "The police took the computer to examine it. I guess they're going to check out what she'd been doing last, check those conversations to see if they can get a lead."

"Anything so far?"

"Nah. Nothing."'

"Where did she set up shop with the computer? Do you have a home office?"

"Yeah, we got a small office back here."

Leonard led the detective back through a small hall and into a square 8´x8´ cupboard of a room that housed a basic office desk and a file cabinet on which sat a printer. A clean rectangle was outlined in the dust on the desk where the computer had once sat.

Leonard waved at the office. "Well, here it is."

Chase browsed around, opening drawers and looking behind furniture. He shook his head, knowing how little there was to search through because the police had probably grabbed anything of relevance. If there was anything they had overlooked, it wouldn't be much at all.

Printer paper, pens, paperclips—it was all a collection of basic office supplies. Other than a couple of sticky notes, there wasn't even anything on which Shelby had written.

DeBarlo turned to Leonard. "Did your wife ever write up some sort of case notes for her investigations?"

The burly man scratched his head. "Well, I don't really know."

"Please think. I ask because, as an investigator myself, I write down notes all the time. I'm not comparing what she does to what I do, but all I'm finding here are a couple sticky notes about household chores."

"Well, the cops did take the computer."

"Yes, but you're saying they didn't find anything on it."

"Well, so far."

"So far."

The two stood in the small office for a long, awkward pause until Leonard's eyes finally lit up. "Well, come to think of it now, I did see her writing in a notebook sometimes—a regular one, you know, bigger than yours."

Chase sighed, naturally impatient at having to walk the man through the brainstorming process, but keeping his cool. "Okay, good. That might be something. Did the police happen to take a notebook out of here like that?"

"No, they only took the computer."

The private investigator pondered his own office setup and the small things he had hidden about back in Fallsbury. While his computer genius friend, Rock Rickman, had assured his digital security, there was something about being connected to the world that Chase simply didn't trust. So he kept a lot of paper copies hidden about, some of the more private ones—he had it!

"In a small home office like this, there's only one real private place I can think of, Mr. Gammel."

Chase bent down in front of the file cabinet and pulled out the bottom-most drawer. As with most file cabinet drawers, it didn't pull out all the way in order to prevent imbalance and the cabinet tipping over. He reached behind and underneath the drawer and discovered, tucked away, a spiral three-subject notebook with a black cover.

DeBarlo held up his find. "Is this the notebook you were talking about?"

"That's the one!"

Chase began leafing through it. "Looks like some sort of journal."

"No, no. You ain't going to be reading through her diary."

The detective held up a hand. "Relax. It's a journal about her ghosthunting."

"Oh yeah? How do you know?"

Chase stepped back into the hall and headed out toward the living room. "Come on. We'll read it together in front of that nice fire you've got going."

November 14

I couldn't believe the weight of the place. Walking into that abandoned, desecrated church was like taking all of its bricks upon my back and trying to trudge through the mud. I've been investigating for about three years now, and this church out at Black Bear is the darkest place I've been to so far.

When you walk in, it feels like all eyes are upon you. You see the shadows peering in through the windows—short, stout shadow figures, just barely taller than the bottom of the windows, boring holes into you. They didn't come in, but they surrounded us. Something else was inside with us.

Cathy first noticed it when we walked up the short set of stairs at the back of the church. She said she thought she saw a shadow darting around the top of the walls

where the roof had been. She took a couple pictures with her digital camera, and we moved on, but we didn't have to move far. Directly to our right, as we reached the top of the stairs, was a concrete platform about waist high with a number of bones strewn atop it. Some of them looked burned and there may have been drops of blood on the concrete, but it was hard to tell with the poor lighting. That's when I thought I first saw the crawler lurking near the top of that little room. I didn't say anything.

Chris and Taylor ventured over to where the altar had once been and tried to get a feel for the area. It was more than 50 degrees out, but I could see their breath. Cathy could see it, too. Mike had gone out to the middle of the church to take pictures of where Chris and Taylor stood and he was suddenly excited. He had caught a brilliant ball of light in one of the pictures he took and kept snapping away. The flash from his camera was like a strobe light, and out of the corner of my eye I could see the slinky shadow crawling around the top of the walls. Cathy raised her own camera and began taking pictures in the direction of the crawler. My EMF detector registered nothing, but all the hair on the back of my neck was raised.

The darkness of the church completely enveloped us. Hadn't this once been a place of worship? It was desecrated now, littered with graffiti and waste, and whatever somebody had conjured up was surrounding us, staring at us, creeping in closer to us. We waited.

Time limped by, but nothing happened. We were deathly quiet, listening for anything our ears or our audio recorders may have been able to pick up. Nothing. Suddenly, a huge gust of wind picked up right in the middle of the church and nearly bowled us over. It had been a completely calm night, but this gust was as if it had been from a large storm. Afterward, it was completely still again, save for the five of us, who were now eying each other over, searching for answers. We stuck around a while longer, but left shortly thereafter.

January 6

We decided to make a day excursion to Black Bear en route to an investigation out in Enid. Our team loves road trips! Thankfully, it wasn't such a cold day for winter.

The church did not seem as menacing during the day and all was quiet. A slight heaviness still hung in the air, but it was nowhere near as prevalent as it had been two months prior. Instead of spending so much time in the church this time, we focused on the cemetery across the dirt road. I can't believe I'm going to say this, but the cemetery "felt" better than the church.

It does seem odd, I know, that a place where the dead are buried would feel lighter and more cheerful than a place where God was once worshiped, but the desecration of the church with whatever rituals had been done in the back must have really overpowered what was once good there.

I had done a little research on the church and the cemetery over the past couple of weeks, but there's not a lot to be found. It was a rural church built for the small community of farmers around it, but it seemed to have fallen out of use around the late 1960s or early 1970s. It was hard to pinpoint it exactly, because there was no official record of the closing. My guess is that with the advent of modern transportation, folks in the area just found it more convenient to drive into town to worship at the bigger congregations. Perhaps there had been some holdovers from those who founded the church, but once they started leaving or passing away, I imagine their spots were just never filled.

Now the building is an absolute wreck, but I'm somehow drawn to it. An alarm in the back of my mind tells me I should just concentrate on who or what may be at the cemetery, but the graves of the original settlers of the area aren't interesting me right now. I want to know what was crawling around that church and what blew the gust of wind at us.

However, our focus for the day was to get a better grasp of the cemetery and then head on further to Enid. And that's what we did.

January 13

I shouldn't have done this, but I went out to Black Bear on my own. One of our rules for the group is that we always investigate with someone else as a matter of protection. But this was an off weekend and I couldn't drum up someone to go with me. This place has been such a draw for me that I had to go, although I don't think my husband was very happy about it.

I'm having a hard time with this experience. I was out there for a couple hours and never saw the crawler, but I was definitely surrounded by something. All through the windows I saw the shadows lurking and peering in. I sat in the middle of the church and even invited them in. I've got to be crazy. That's just inviting trouble.

The strange thing is that they wouldn't come in. These short shadow figures stood outside the windows and just seemingly stared at me with dark recessed sockets for eyes, their really only discernible feature. Sometimes I thought I heard a low hum or a chant come from them, but I saw no mouths on any of them. It was very creepy and uncomfortable, and the church became extremely cold — even colder than it already was!

Like the last time, I got no hits on the EMF detector, but I was doing some burst EVP sessions and got a few responses that were extremely unnerving. When I introduced myself and asked for a name, I received a series of guttural sounds. When I asked what they wanted, the response over the audio recorder was, "Get out." Typical. But the third one really got to me. In the third one, they called out both my name and my husband's! That made all of this very personal.

Even with that, I stayed a little while longer, but I didn't capture anything else over my audio recorder. I did capture a few photographs of small illuminated balls of light, similar to the large one Mike had taken a few weeks ago. Most of these hung over the area in which the altar had once been and a few were hovering around the windows. The largest, moving in an upward direction, was taken coming up out of the stairwell that leads to the small basement.

I only left because I told myself I'd only be there for a couple hours, otherwise I would have stayed there the night, even with how cold it was starting to get. It was an act of discipline that was challenging to maintain. As much as my nerves were racked about being out there on my own, I was completely fascinated by what was going on around the walls of the church.

January 15

Now I'm scared. I knew I shouldn't have gone out to Black Bear on my own and now I think something is in my house. I've never had this happen before, but lights have been turning on and off around the house and ceiling fans have been turning on, on their own. I even caught the scent of a foul stench in the living room from out of nowhere.

I don't want to tell my husband about it. Even if he believed me, he would give me some sort of "I told you so" remark, since he's never really liked me being a paranormal investigator. What am I going to do?

Leonard stared into the fire and didn't say anything for a full minute. Finally, he sighed and turned to Chase. "I wish she would have told me. It's not that I don't believe her that these paranormal things happen; I just don't think she's careful enough. I guess I was right. I can't believe she went out there on her own! I remember that day. She told me she was going to her sister's."

Chase wasn't about to get into the domestic issues of a wife who has lied to her husband about where she was going, so he stuck to the case. "Can you put me in touch with this paranormal team? You said it was called Society of the Haunted?"

"You have to understand, I don't think dabbling around with the deceased is a smart thing to do. We don't know what's really out there, and there have been too many stories I've heard lately of evil entities taking control of a home. I don't know if all of that stuff is true, but I'm not going to take that kind of chance."

"Mr. Gammel, I'm not here to debate whether this paranormal stuff is true or not; I really don't know if it is. I'm just here to find your wife. Maybe this group has some sort of clue about her whereabouts, and maybe they can show me this church she became attached to."

The church really was out in the middle of nowhere. Chase found himself bounding down a dusty dirt road in an old, blue Chevy Astro Van surrounded by strangers in black t-shirts on a seemingly endless journey to parts unknown. Their conversation during the hour-and-a-half long ride was littered with ghosts, eccentric clients, and out-of-the-way diner tales. The private investigator from New England wasn't sure if he'd ever make it back to some sort of legitimate civilization.

When they finally pulled into the small dirt drive of the church, it was just as Shelby had described in her journal. The building was small and decrepit, devoid of its roof, brush was growing tall around it, and graffiti was scrawled out on every wall. Chase liked old buildings and history, and he was rather anxious to venture inside, even with the desecration.

Vanessa, the team's auburn-haired psychic, remarked from the back of the van, "Oh, I don't like this place."

Chase turned around to face her as Mike parked the van. "You've never been here?"

"I usually remote view into the investigations instead of actually going out with the group, but since Shelby is missing, I thought I ought to come out this time. The feel of this place is all wrong."

Chase had no idea what "remote view" meant, and he wasn't sure he wanted to. Much of what they had been discussing throughout the trip was foreign to him, ramblings of an eclectic collection of people that must have had a few screws loose.

Just before the van halted, Cathy, the team's case manager, jumped out of the side door and ran to the front entrance of the church yelling, "Shelby!"

In the passenger's seat, Chris exhaled, "Alrighty. Glad she didn't hurt herself."

Once the van came to a complete stop, the rest of the troop piled out and stretched their legs. Various group members opened the rear doors of the vehicle and grabbed equipment bags while Chase followed Cathy's footsteps into the church. He blew through the short entrance hall and into the small open sanctuary of the church, but he did not see the woman they were looking for. His eyes darted about the details of the desecrated church, absorbing the details of what once had been a place of worship. All the windows had been broken out, but he didn't spot any shadowy figures peering at him from beyond as described in Shelby's journal. He only saw the green foliage of the brush that had grown tall around the building. Piles of junk containing remnants of the roof, sticks, and bits of trash from wayward visitors were strewn about the floor. Charred embers of a small fire rested in the center of the sanctuary, but Chase quickly dismissed it as something that had burned quite a long time ago and not recently by Shelby—if this was where she had really gone.

Cathy finally emerged from a small stairwell on the far right side of the church and she shook her head. "She's not down there."

Chase climbed the small set of four stairs directly to the left of the ones Cathy had just ascended, and found himself in a small room with a raised stone slab to his right. The slab seemed to be originally just a part of the building's construction, but he saw that it had been used for other purposes afterward. The slab had been charred in the manner of someone lighting small fires atop it, and a few small bones were strewn about its surface.

Cathy appeared beside him. "That's where we think they were practicing the occult."

Chase nodded. "You just left the bones sitting here?"

"Would you want to touch them?"

"I suspect not."

Cathy turned and walked back down the stairs. "I took one home."

A sudden call shrilled across the air and the two bolted out of the church. The rest of the group had ventured across the dirt road to the cemetery and Taylor was waving them to the stand of trees that sprouted out of the middle of the acre of headstones. They sprinted across, through the wide front gate, to the spot where the group was huddled around a figure on the ground.

"W-what am I doing here?" asked a very shaken Shelby Gammel.

The paranormal team smiled and hugged their friend.

Private investigator Chase Michael DeBarlo propped up his feet on the large oak desk in his office in Fallsbury, Massachusetts, and was just starting to unwind. Part of his process was drinking a late coffee and perusing through email, usually a simple mundane task, but within this night's collection of spam was an email from an undisclosed recipient with the subject line, "Fire."

Within the message content was an article from *The Oklahoman*, the large newspaper out of Oklahoma City, titled, "Husband and wife perish in inferno." He shook his head and sighed when he read that the blaze had claimed the lives of Leonard and Shelby Gammel. His client would be saddened and was sure he'd hear of it from her soon. Chase closed the email and took a sip of his coffee.

From out of the corner of his eye, the detective thought he saw a shadow dart from one corner of his office to the other.

He placed down his mug. "Nah. It's just an old ghost story."

The Midwest is rife with paranormally active locations. What you've just read are but a handful of ghost stories at a few highlighted locations. There is so much more to be found—perhaps right in your own backyard. Is it a historic haunt or a former murder scene? Is it a creepy cemetery with spectral visitors that once roamed the earth? Perhaps it's a local legend with some grains of truth that frighten the community. I encourage you, dear reader, to begin your own research and discover what else may lurk throughout the shadows of the Midwest.